OPEN ROADS

By

James L. Edwards

This book is a work of fiction. Places, events, and situations in this story are purely fictional. Any resemblance to actual persons, living or dead, is coincidental.

ISBN: 0-7596-9840-6

This book is printed on acid free paper.

1st Books - rev. 3/28/02

Chapter 1

I had been struggling all day on writing that I nearly forgot that Josh was taking me out for my birthday tonight. I realized it was 4:00 p.m. and remembered that Josh would be here soon, which left little time for a shower. Josh and I had been friends for almost twelve years and we knew everything about each other. He was more intelligent than he let on; Josh scored highly on his S.A.T test, but never wanted to be treated any different. It was a friendship that few people could say they had, but wish they did. Josh said he planned on going to medical school to become a doctor, me well I enjoyed my writing and wasn't sure how to use it to my advantage. I had been working on my first novel with little success and recalled what Josh always told me, "You'll make a great writer someday, take your time and it will come." With that, I put my work aside for the night.

Time was growing shorter, and I was really behind I knew I wouldn't be ready in time and had to hurry. Jim, My mother yelled from downstairs, Josh will be here soon. I know, I just have to take a quick shower, I said as I finished getting undressed and grabbed a towel around my waist. The doorbell rang and I ran down stairs to answer it, I knew it was Josh and I wanted to explain why I was late. " Come on in I'm sort of running behind", I said. " Happy Birthday", he said as he entered. " Thanks, I'm really sorry, I lost track of the time", I said. " How's the writing coming along?" he asked. " How'd you know that was the reason I'm late?" I said surprised. " You always work on it to hard." Josh said. " Well your right, I was and I'll be ready soon." I said. "Take your time, no need to rush. Have a little confidence, you'll find the words in time." Josh said in a reassuring manner. "I hope your right, Sometimes I feel I'll never succeed, Its really frustrating, maybe I should just give up." I said. "You and I both know that is not the answer, you can do it, I believe in you." Josh said out of concern. "Maybe tonight will help with your writers block, Just relax and enjoy the night." He said. "By the way where are we going?" I asked. "You'll see, go take your shower, I've got to talk to your mother." Josh said as he went to the kitchen.

"I thought you might like to see what I got Jim for his birthday," Josh said as he held out a case with a gold chain with a bolt of lightening attached. " Do you think he'll like it?" "I'm sure he will, all he's done is talk about wanting a gold chain." My mother told him. "How much did it set you back?" she asked. " It cost a few pay checks, but it's worth it for a friend." " So, where are you two off to tonight?" she said. "Well, I thought we'd play some pool and maybe get a bite to eat." Just be careful. " Is it alright if I stay over tonight?" Josh asked with hesitation in his voice, My parents said if I'm too late they'll lock me out." "Sure, why don't you have a key?" my mother asked out of concern. " They took it away and said I can't become a doctor if I'm out late." Josh said. "Your always home by 9:00 p.m., why do they think it's to late?" " My parents don't approve of any thing I do unless I do everything their way." He said. "I wanted to stay out late with Jim on his birthday, I thought he'd like spending it with a friend." "If you have to be in at a certain time Jim won't mind." My mother said to him. "I know, but I would Its his birthday and Its a special night for him." "You know your always welcome here Josh, you don't need to ask." "Thanks I won't stay to late in the morning." Josh said with a sign of relief in his voice. "Don't worry about it, stay as long as you want." She said. " Just don't tell Jim about my parents, I don't want him worrying about me while he's working on his book." Josh said. "He needs to concentrate on what he's doing." "Okay, but if your friends I think you should tell him." She said. "I will another time. Thanks again." said Josh as he headed upstairs.

I heard Josh enter my room, so I finished up and turned off the shower. "I'll be right out, have a seat if you want." I yelled through the door. "How's the book coming along anyway ", he said as he picked up a copy off my desk and started to read it. "Slow, I really got a bad case of writers block, I think the story itself is junk." Josh, reading my story said. " I like it and I think the rest of the world will too. I told you before it takes patience to do this kind of work and it will pay off, trust yourself it will work out." He said. Drying off, I realized Josh was right as usual. Somehow he always knew me better than I knew myself. I wish I had the kind of confidence that he had in me myself. I quickly put on my pants and left the bathroom to go to my room. Josh, feeling caught put my book down as if I didn't notice him reading it. "Its okay you can read it if you want to." "Are you sure, I mean I didn't think you'd want anyone reading it." He said apologetically. "You already started so you might as well finish reading what I got so far." I said. "I'll have time later, I'm staying here tonight." He said in anticipation. "Great, then I guess this will be one hell of a night to remember after all." "I told you it would, I never lie about things like that." Josh said excitedly.

"By the way Josh, I hope you haven't forgotten about our trip to New Hampshire this summer, have you?" I asked him. " Not at all, I'm looking forward to it." "It's really not that far off and we still have to plan it out in more detail. Maybe we'll have some time tonight Josh after we get back." I said. Josh sat back in the chair reading my book as I finished getting ready; "I was right about your writing." He paused. "What do you mean by that." I asked. "I think you have talent and you shouldn't sell yourself short. Do you realize by giving up you risk never knowing how good you really are?" he said to me. "I know, but it seems like I can't always find the words I'm looking for." I said to him. Concentrating on the final paragraph, "Jim you owe it to yourself to finish this book, eventually the words will come, but for now let's just have fun." He said. Josh was one person I could always count on and maybe that's what made our friendship so tight. We could do nothing but hang out listening to tunes and still be the best of friends.

We started downstairs before I realized I forgot my jacket, " Josh I'll be right back." I said as I ran back upstairs. "Now what did you forget?" he said. "My jacket, you now I never leave home without it." I said laughing. " Its eighty degrees out are you nuts, you don't need a jacket." He yelled. " It's my trade mark, sort of like your pendant is yours." I told him. "I'm not going to argue I'll wait downstairs, Besides, my pendant is a necklace not a jacket there is a big difference." He said in a harsh voice. "Maybe to you, but not me." I said as I headed back to my room.

Let's go, yelled Josh from downstairs. I grabbed my jacket and put it on as I ran downstairs, "Okay I'm ready." I said out of breath. "Your so dam slow sometimes." Josh said. "Yeah, but I'm never late for anything am I?" I said. "You got me there," Josh laughed. " So, what are we doing tonight anyway." I asked. "I thought we'd play some pool." Josh said as he opened the door. "Sounds good to me, But I'm not that great, you always beat me." I said. "It's not about who wins all the time, besides, all the cues suck, so," he said as he reached behind the seat, "this is gift number one." He pulled out a long black case and handed it to me, I was shocked and without words, I didn't expect anything. " Well open it, what are you waiting for?" Josh said excitedly. "Josh, You didn't have to do this." I said. "I know, but birthdays only come around once a year." I opened it and was amazed; "It's your own cue stick, like mine." Josh said. "Thanks, It's great." I said. "Now your ready to play a real game against me, and maybe this time you'll win." Josh said with confidence. As we pulled out of my driveway I remembered his last words, "What do you mean gift one, what exactly are you up to?" "Laughing, Josh said, "You'll see later, Right now it's party time." Josh reached for a tape and put it in the tape deck.

We drove to the pool hall and listened to the music, which made me realize how lucky I really was, nothing would ruin the night ahead. Josh sat there singing to himself and I just laughed. Josh reached for the volume turning it down and said, "What's so funny?" "Nothing, I just can't picture you as a singer, let alone able to hold a tune." I said laughing. "Oh, and you can do better." Josh said. " I never said I could sing and I know you can't." I said to him. " I guess I can't can I.," he said laughing. He reached for the volume and turned it back up, with that we both made fools out of ourselves and sang completely off key. We drove in silence, just listening to the music and thinking about what lay ahead. Josh told me he had been planning this night for sometime, he said that a person should never be alone on their birthday, it should be spent with friends. I never questioned anything he really did, because I knew there was always a reason. I also knew that our friendship would last a lifetime.

" So, why are you staying over tonight?" I asked. "Well, my parents said if I plan on staying out late don't come home tonight." He answered. "What do mean?" I asked confused. "They don't believe a future doctor should be out, he should be studying instead." He said. I could almost hear the hurt in his voice because of the way his parents treated him. "We don't need to be out late, it's really not that important." "It's your birthday, I've never forgotten it before, and I do not plan on starting now. Besides, don't you want me to stay over?" Josh said to me. "Yeah, but that's not the point." "What is your point then?" Josh asked. "I wouldn't want you to get into trouble because of me." "Look, Don't worry about it, I can deal with it." He said as if hiding something. "If you say so, I won't even mention it again." I said with my fingers crossed. "Great, because it's to depressing anyway." Josh replied. We finally arrived at the pool hall minutes later and I couldn't believe all the cars in the parking lot. "I guess everyone had the same idea tonight." I said as I stared at all the cars.

Josh finally found a parking spot, right next to a familiar car we both recognized. "Josh, I thought Dave had to go away this week." "Maybe plans changed at the last minute," he said as he shut off the car. I opened the door and Josh reminded me to grab my stick. Oh yeah, I almost forgot. " I'll show you how to put it together inside." He told me as he got out of the car. I was preoccupied with trying to figure out why Dave never bothered to let us know that his plans changed. "What's on your mind," Josh asked as we walked to the entrance. " I was just wondering why Dave never bothered to call us." I told him. "I'm sure he has a reason, just ask him inside." Josh said to me. " It's not like him at all to just ignore us like that." Smiling, Josh said, "I'm sure you'll soon know why."

The lights were really dim, so dim in fact that we couldn't see the back tables at all. We made our way to the attendant and I noticed Josh hand him an extra twenty-dollar bill. "Why did you pay him now?" I asked him. "Just to make sure we can keep our table longer. Let's play back there, we can have more room so you can concentrate on the game." He said. I started walking towards the back, about twenty or more people yelled, surprise! I stood there for a moment until it all sank in. I turned to Josh; "You did this didn't you?" I replied. Laughing, Josh said, "We'll, I might have had something to do with this." " I can't believe this, thanks guys." I said to him. "I told you it would be a night to remember, didn't I?" josh said with a smile. "Everyone from our class is here, how did you pull this off." I said as I stood in shock. "It wasn't exactly that difficult, I called everyone a couple of nights ago and told them." He answered. "Happy Birthday Jim, Now let the fun begin. Let's get some music, this is a party people." He shouted to the guy at the jukebox. I never realized how many friends I really had until this instant.

"So, what's it like to be eighteen," Josh said as he opened his pool stick case. " I'm not sure, I don't feel any older." I answered. "Good, age is only a number, It's all in how you feel." Josh reassured me. Dave made his way over and held out his hand. "Happy Birthday Jim, I'm sorry I lied to you but as you can see, I had a reason." "It's cool, I'm glad to see everyone. I really appreciate this, thanks again." "No problem, it was worth it to see the look on your face," Josh said as he laughed. I still couldn't believe what everyone had gone through for me that night, I always thought I never had any friends. Somehow this night changed the way I saw others. "Jim, come on let's put your stick together and play." Josh yelled from across the room. I always knew Josh and I was friends, tonight reinforced my belief.

The music played loudly, some danced others played pool with their friends while, some just talked with each other. I still couldn't believe my eyes; no one ever did anything like this for me before. I decided Josh was right, it was time to play. "Okay Jim, First take out the pieces and screw them together like this." Josh demonstrated. As I attempted to follow his lead I found myself overwhelmed by the atmosphere in the room. "Now you got it, in honor of your birthday let's play for real." Josh said. I felt like I was on top of the world and nothing else mattered.

I watched as Josh racked up the balls, and thought to myself how lucky I was to have such a great friend. "Do you want to break, or should I?" Josh asked. " Maybe you'd better, breaking isn't exactly my best shot remember?" I said laughing. As Josh took his position I watched trying to learn every move I could not realizing I had already learned from the best. The shot sunk two stripes and he scratched leaving me with an open shot for three solids lined perfectly. "Thanks for the great set up, but with my luck I'll miss completely." I said. "Concentrate on the shot and line it up, like this." Josh demonstrated. " See it's just a matter of lining up your shot before you shoot. Pool is just like math class, all angles." Josh explained to me. I took my shot and surprised myself as I sunk all three balls without sinking the white. "Great shot Jim, I knew you could do it. Now look at the table find your next shot." Josh said excitedly. Confidence was one thing I lacked and never really had in myself; it felt good that someone had faith in me even if it wasn't me. The music played loudly in the background and I could almost feel the rhythm flowing through me like a sense of power.

I took my next shot and missed, but not without blocking Josh's shot maybe it wasn't a bad shot afterall I thought to myself. "Let's see you sink that one." I said with an attitude. "Oh, and you think that will stop me, Watch this hotshot." He said as he took aim and shot at the opposite corner. I watched in amazement as he banked and hit that ball I blocked without touching my ball. I couldn't believe my eyes, I thought to myself and noticed Josh smiled with a devilish grin. "I told you I wasn't going to hold back, so I'd make every shot count if I were you." Josh said with a grin. Josh took aim at a perfect shot that would sink all but two balls he had left, which in turn left me without a prayer unless he scratched. I watched in anticipation as he took aim and shot, with almost perfect accuracy and scratched on the third ball. I only had to sink four balls which was next to impossible for someone as bad as me. "Remember what I told you, look for your shot and line each shot up" Josh said trying to help. "I thought you weren't going to help me anymore?" I said. "I still want you to learn as we play, I never meant to imply that I wouldn't help guide you. You're the one that has to shot not me." Josh replied. "Thanks, not just for the help but for all of this." I said. "No sweat, I figured your eighteenth birthday should be one you never forget. Now line up your shot so you can set yourself up for the next shot without over shooting." Josh said in a helpful way. "Yeah right, Here goes nothing." I said. But before I could shot Josh reached out and stopped me. "I don't want to here that kind of negative attitude from you, have confidence in all your shots do you got me?" Josh said with anger in his voice. I stood in a state of shock, Josh and I never raised our voices at each other before, and I felt incredibly stupid at that moment.

"What did I do wrong." I asked. " Look just stop feeling sorry for yourself and have confidence in what ever you do, I'm not going to be around forever to help you." Josh said emotionally. "I didn't know you were that serious about what I do." I replied frustrated. "You can do anything you want as long as you apply yourself, it's the same with your writing have confidence in what you can do and you'll never fail as long as you try." Josh said as if he were my father. "No one fails as long as they try to do their best, don't ever let me hear you talk like that again, Now take your shot with confidence, hit or miss it doesn't matter as long as you try." Josh replied. With that I took careful aim, and made my shot sinking the ball and setting myself up for another perfect shot. "Great shot, Now line up your next shot carefully." Josh said excitedly. I took aim and noticed that I could sink two with one shot if I did it correctly, and took that chance with success, leaving one final ball left.

Josh stood there as though he knew all along that I could do it, which made me feel like I was the luckiest human being on the face of the planet. I took aim at what was the most difficult shot of my life, and sunk it and the white ball. "You did great Jim, I knew you could do it." Josh reassured me. "But I scratched and may have cost myself the game." I replied sadly. "The games not over yet, I can still miss the eight ball and you could win." He said. As I watched Josh aim, and call his shot to the corner, couldn't help the fact that I hoped he'd miss. Josh shot the cue ball perfectly into the eight ball sending down slowly to the corner pocket for a perfect shot. "I told you the game was over." I said. " Yeah, but you just played your best game ever, this was the closest you've ever come to beating me, how's it feel?" Josh asked. "It feels great, how about a rematch?" I said to him. "No problem. But first, how about you open your gifts from the rest of your friends?" Josh said with excitement in his voice. "Everyone gather around so Jim can open his gifts." Josh shouted. The party itself was a surprise, but I didn't expect anything else. I tried to sneak away but was quickly caught by Josh. "Where do you think your going?" Josh shouted out loud. "Haven't you done enough, I mean the party, the pool stick, you didn't have to go through all this trouble for me." I replied. "The party's just getting started and you're trying to duck out, You haven't seen anything yet Jim." Josh said laughing. Everyone gathered around me like a mob trying to capture a criminal and I realized I had no other choice but to surrender to the crowd. Josh stood there as if he were the leader of a gang; his expression scared me but at the same time made me wonder what else was to come.

The crowd stared waiting for me to make the next move even though the choice was already made for me by Josh. Before I could say anything, someone stepped forward, Dave to be exact, and handed me a package. "Go ahead open it, Lisa and I picked it out for you." Dave said nervously. "We're all here for you Jim, Birthday's like this one only come around once in a life time." Josh said. "Then let's party, Josh." I replied finally. "Now that's the spirit, Someone play some tunes and let's really get this party started!" Josh shouted. I figured I wasn't getting out of this one too easily, so I might as well join in, afterall it was a party. Josh had a way of being very convincing when it came to something he thought was right. In fact, he was right a birthday should be spent with great friends the memories one shares with others will never be forgotten.

I opened the package and looked inside, I couldn't believe my eyes, two tickets to the upcoming rock festival in August. "You like it, We thought you and Josh might want to go with us." Dave said excitedly. "It's great, We'll both be there." I said. I looked at Josh and felt like I had been in the dark about everything around me that night. I found myself realizing that I underestimated Josh all these years. Josh whispered something into Eric's ear, something I couldn't quite make out, but knew he was up to something. Eric left the room, and headed towards the front of the building, which of course I lost complete sight of him. Where's Eric off to in such a hurry Josh?" I asked. "He'll be back soon, he had to go get something at home." Josh replied. Everyone seemed to crowd around me waiting to see what else I received from my friends. I kept wondering to myself what other surprises Josh had in store for me that night. Josh always went to the extreme on everything he planned; he always had to top his last feat.

As the crowd around me grew greater, I noticed that Josh slipped into the next room that was when I knew he was up to something. I opened gift after gift amazed at how many friends I really did have that night. Josh, came out of the front room smiling at me as though we first met, as if trying to cover something up. "Josh, what are you doing over there, I thought we were here to party?" I asked him. "I had to make a phone call, Don't worry the party's just getting started." Josh replied quickly. Josh was never a good liar, I could always see right through his expressions. I turned my attention to a card someone had placed in front of me, I opened it and began to read, *Happy Birthday to someone I've known for years and was always there when I needed him, open the door in front of you and turn on the light!*

Signed a friend

"Okay, Who wrote this one?" I asked. Before I could get an answer, I heard a voice over the loud speaker that I really recognized. "Open the door and find out." The voice said. "Mike, is that you?" I said as I opened the door. Behind the door, Josh arranged for our friend to put on a concert for all of us. Mike and his band stood there waiting to play. "Happy Birthday Jim, Let's really party." Mike said as he began to play. I turned to Josh who stood beside me and smiled for I knew this was indeed a birthday I would never forget.

Mike had been playing music since he was eight years old, he even taught himself how to play. He had released many C.D's, all of which he had supplied lead vocals. I knew one day he would make it big because he had just signed to a major record label and was in fact well on his way to success. The music was a mix of hard rock and heavy metal, all of which appealed to the entire crowd. Watching him up on stage I wondered what it was like to perform in front of a large crowd of people. Before I could even finish my thought, Mike came down and pulled me onto the stage, by force of course. I stood there in front of everyone, and saw my dreams become reality. It felt like the whole world stopped and all eyes were on us, something few people get a chance to experience. As I left the stage, I looked into his eyes and thanked him without words; it actually felt great to have all my friends together that night. "Wishes do come true, If you really want them to Jim." Josh said to me.

As Mike played, I could only think of how perfect this birthday was, I only wish the night would never end. It was around 11.00 when the party started to die down, and people began to say good-bye. I knew some I would see at school and some I would never see for quite some time, but we were all still close friends no matter where we would end up. I walked over to Josh and still couldn't believe what he had done for me. "Josh, can I talk to you in private?" I asked. "Sure what's up Jim?" he said as he excused himself from a group of our friends. "I wanted to thank you, for all of this it was really incredible. It meant a lot to me and I know you went through a lot of trouble." I stated. "It was my pleasure, believe me. Bye the way, How do you feel?" Josh asked me. "What do you mean?" I replied. "What I mean is how's your writers block?" he asked me. For the first time in a long time, I actually didn't think at all about my work. "I feel relaxed and even at ease about a lot of things." I told him. Josh put his hand on my shoulder and I felt at ease as though nothing else really mattered. "Good for you, I told you all you needed was a little time to yourself. Maybe now your writing will come to you easier." Josh said to me as we helped Mike pack his equipment.

A part of me was still in shock; I never had a birthday party like the one tonight, which made me feel popular for the first time. "We definitely have to party more often, This was one hell of a night." Mike said. "Don't worry, We still have the whole summer ahead of us." Josh answered. "Well, after you and I get back from our trip, or have you forgotten your promise?" I asked Josh. "Hell No! I wouldn't forget about that, besides tonight we make plans. I never go back on my word." Josh stated to me. I had always been insecure about everything all my life, and I should've realized that my friends would never go back on their promises they make to me. I never felt like I belonged anywhere, even with them sometimes, perhaps in time all that will change. I finished loading Mike's truck and waited outside for Josh and Mike, The moon was full that night and I remembered some one once told me when the moon is full and bright your cycle is complete and all your dreams will come true. Josh and Mike came out with the guitars and cords; I stood there and daydreamed about how perfect life was for that one moment. "Hey wake up over there, You alright?" Josh yelled to me. "Word's can't always describe a great night like this." I said to them both.

We sat on the back of Mike's truck for awhile just drinking our soda and talking, the kind of talk guys do. "I couldn't have asked for a better night guys. Thanks for everything." I said to them. "Who said the night's over, you and I still have something else to do." Josh replied. "What about you Mike, Where are you off to tonight?" I asked. "I have a concert out of state tomorrow and I'm leaving tonight." Mike answered. "Well, thanks for playing tonight I really enjoyed it." I said. We hopped of the back of the truck, and Mike put the tailgate up, I finished my soda and tossed it in the trash. "Well, I guess I'll see you guys when I get back." Mike said to us. "How long you going on this tour for." I asked him as he got in the truck. "Well, I figure at least four weeks, maybe more it all depends on how well we pack them in." Mike replied as he closed the door. "Good luck and thanks again for everything." I said to him as he drove off. I turned to Josh and he was smiling like I did something to make him laugh. "What are you laughing at; You know, I'm beginning to get very nervous when you look at me like that." I told him.

I learned that I should never underestimate Josh, somehow he always had something else up his sleeve. "I told you the night's not over yet." Josh said laughing. We started to walk to the car and I still had no idea what he was up to. "Josh everyone's gone what else is there to do?" I asked him as we got in the car. "I want to take you somewhere that you've never been before, I think you'll actually like this place it helps me to clear my head, maybe it will become your place as well." Josh said. I never knew all Josh's hang out's, even close friends do indeed have secrets from each other and I was surprised that he decided to share one of them with me. I think at that point Josh and I became closer friends than we ever were. As we were driving, Josh had told me that this place was a popular place that he went anytime that he needed to get away from the everyday world. The ride was long and I had no idea where we were going, I was only told to sit back and enjoy the ride. We played Mike's new tape that he gave us at the party, he told us it wasn't even released yet and that we were the first to each get a copy of the finished product. Even though we heard two of the songs, there were still ten others never released yet. "So, where are we going this time?" I asked him. " Just wait were almost there." Josh said in anticipation.

The night was warm and the road we traveled didn't have any streetlights all I did notice was the smell of salt water. "Why are we at the beach at this time of night, I thought the beach was closed?" I asked him. "It is closed, no lifeguard, but that doesn't mean people can't come here to sit or walk on the beach." Josh said. "Besides, I still have to give you one more gift. I wanted to give it to you in private." Josh replied. We parked the car and Josh asked if I wanted to go for a walk on the beach. I myself have never been to the beach; I couldn't swim so I had no real reason to go to the beach. Josh was the swimmer; in fact, he was on the swim team in high school and enjoyed swimming as a way to relax. I never learned because I was always afraid of the water. Josh had offered many times to teach me, I always backed out because of my fear; I thought I would always have time to learn later. "Yeah, I don't see any harm in that, unless you're planning on drowning me?" I said jokingly. "I told you when your ready to learn I'm ready to teach, Besides that's not why I brought you here." Josh told me. "Then why did you?" I asked. "I thought you would like the beach, maybe get a feel for it the way I do. I also wanted to give you something in private." Josh said. "You've already done enough for me, what else is there?" I asked. Before I could finish the question, Josh held out a small box and handed it to me. "Open it." He said as we walked. "Josh, Why are you doing all of this, the party itself was more than enough." I told him. I opened the box and in it was a gold chain with a lightning bolt. "Josh, thanks a lot. How can you afford such a gift like this?" I asked him. "You like it. I thought it was about time you wore a real good chain." Josh said. "You know I do. It's the best gift I ever got." I answered.

The beach was actually crowded for being closed, I never realized that people came after hours. I decided to walk barefoot, the air and sand was actually cool which made it a perfect night. The full moon made the water glow as if it were daylight. I put the chain on and gazed at the pendant, still not able to believe what everyone had done for me that night. “So, Do you like it or what?” Josh asked me. “Yes, I really do.” I said. “Then what’s wrong, You haven’t said much.”Josh asked concerned. “No one’s ever done anything like this for me, why did you?” I asked. “I wanted you to have a great birthday, a real party with people that are your friends, even if you didn’t realize how many you have.” Josh stated. Josh stopped walking and turned towards me suddenly. “You have more friends than you realize, don’t shut them out. I’m not always going to be around and I want you to be able to live your life even if I’m not there to share everything with you.” Josh said. That was the first time I felt like we were distant, like our lives were taking different paths and we would walk down separate roads.

We walked for awhile in silence, just watching the waves roll in I couldn’t help but wish I knew how to swim. The water itself seemed warm as it rolled up across my feet. Josh laughed as a huge wave took me by surprise knocking me down and getting me soaked in the process. “I suppose you think that’s funny, don’t you?” I replied. “Didn’t you see it coming? Look at it this way at least you don’t have to take another shower.” Josh laughed. I sat there soaked and began to laugh myself, I couldn’t believe I was that blind. “I guess it is pretty funny, isn’t it?” I said. Josh reached out his hand and I in turn pulled him into the next wave coming at the both of us. I caught only a glimpse of the surprise look on his face before the wave knocked into the two of us. We both sat there just laughing and I thought of how stupid we must look in front of everyone. I stopped laughing long enough to see another huge wave heading directly for us giving me just seconds to get out of the way while Josh got yet another soaking. “Now who’s blind?” I asked him as he looked up at me laughing. “Now that was a rush!” Josh shouted as he got to his feet. “I hope you have a towel in the car, or we’ll be riding home soaked.” I asked. “Who care’s about a towel, that was incredible. Seeing as how were already soaked let’s go in.” Josh said before remembering I couldn’t swim. I turned and started towards the upper beach and felt even more embarrassed than I ever felt in my life. Josh ran up behind me and tried to get my attention, which wasn’t exactly easy being barefoot on rocky ground. He grabbed my shoulder and stopped me in mid step. “Jim, I forgot. I’m really sorry. I’ll teach you how to swim, it’s not that hard I swear." Josh said. I sat down and looked him in the eyes and actually felt ashamed of myself. "Want to learn, but I'm too afraid. I feel like a fool for not knowing how to swim. I lose out on all the fun and can only watch while everyone else has a good time and I'm stuck on the sidelines." I said shivering. "It's okay, one day when you're ready to learn to swim I'll be there to teach you. No one has to know, I promise." Josh replied to me.

We slowly walked back to the car; both of us dripping wet. I turned to Josh and looked at him thinking why he even stayed my friend for all these years. "Josh, Do you think I'm a loser?" I asked him. "No. What ever gave you an idea like that?" He said. "Well, because I can't swim. Does that make me a loser?" I asked him. "You're not a loser. For some people, it takes longer to learn. Give it time, you'll learn when you are ready to learn." Josh said as he threw me a towel. We dried off as best as we could, neither of us had dry clothes with us. We left as we came, with the radio playing. Josh turned on the heat low enough to dry us off a bit so we wouldn't drip water on the floor when we got back to my house. I sat quietly reflecting on everything that day and wished it never would end. We drove back to my house; Josh and I both knew that we still had to plan our trip. We decided to take the long way home, for us it was only an extra ten minutes.

CHAPTER 2

By the time we arrived at my house, it was around twelve a.m., Josh pulled in the driveway and turned off the engine. "Did you enjoy your birthday?" Josh asked as we got out of the car. "Yeah, it was great. I only wish night's like this never ended." I replied heading towards the door. " I know what you mean, I had a great time too. We always manage to make every night great." Josh said. I turned on the downstairs light so we could see where we were going, hoping not to wake anyone up. "Are you sure it's not a problem with me staying over tonight?" Josh asked. "Don't worry, I told you that you can stay anytime. You're a part of this family too, besides my mother wouldn't have it any other way." I told him. We sat on the stairs for a moment before heading upstairs. "Do still want to map out our trip or would you rather do it in the morning?" I asked him. "Let's just sit up for awhile and talk, we can map it out in the morning." Josh replied yawning. I knew we wouldn't be up to long, this was probably the first night in a long time that Josh stayed out late. I knew how strict his parents were, and I knew that Josh did all of this for me. I felt bad that his parents treated him the way they did. I guess some people never think about others the way Josh does. "Let's grab a soda and go upstairs, That is if you can keep you're eyes open long enough." I said. "Sounds good to me, I could use a cold drink." Josh answered. I went into the kitchen and quickly grabbed the sodas and when I returned Josh was standing up ready to go. I handed him his soda and we went up to my room as quietly as possible.

I kept thinking to myself how Josh's parents could treat him the way they did, they seemed like nice people but I guess one never truly knows what goes on behind closed doors. I always liked his parents, and I thought I knew them better than I did. I realize that all people wear masks, maybe a way to hide the truth from others that they do not want to be known. I hope that Josh and I trusted each other enough so that we could always tell each other the truth. Sometimes, I guess it is necessary that some secrets be kept from others maybe in order to protect them from being hurt. "Do you want the bed or the floor?" I asked him. "I'll take the floor, it's your room." Josh said to me. I sat on the bed and Josh pulled up a chair, neither of us was really as tired as let on. “Thanks again for letting me stay over, I appreciate it. I hope I’m not putting you out or anything.” Josh replied yawning. “It’s no problem. Thanks for the great party. I guess that sort of makes us even then.” I said to him. “I guess it does. You really did well at pool tonight, you even came close to beating me and no one’s ever come that close before.” Josh said excitedly. “Well, I had a great teacher and I learned a lot by watching you play in your league.” I stated. “A few more games like tonight, and you may be able to join my league, it would be great to play on the same team again just like in school.” Josh said seriously. “I don’t know if I’m that ready to join a league, I still have a lot to learn. Besides, I thought the league was full?” I asked. “There’s always room for another good player. All you need to do is concentrate on each shot and watch the whole table for your best shot.” Josh replied. I never thought I was good enough to play on a league, but maybe if I practiced more with Josh I could join.

Playing pool was like a rush; to me I could let go of the outside world as if it didn’t exist. I lost myself in each shot just as I did in my writing and it felt very relaxing, so relaxing that nothing else mattered around me. I enjoyed the game as well as the challenge that faced me each time I played. I never felt so free like I did that night, and I never wanted to lose that feeling as long as I lived, It was one memory that couldn’t be replaced. Josh had taught me to play for many hours and showed me almost every possible shot that could be made, so in a way I was prepared as long as I looked at each angle of the table. “Do you really think I’m good enough or are you just playing games with me?” I asked him straight out. “I know your good enough now, we’ve played countless games and you can read each shot better than you could before. I would never have said it if I didn’t think you could do it. The next league starts in September, so that still gives us plenty of practice time. After that you can sign up and see if you can qualify.” Josh said with excitement in his voice. We drank our sodas and just sat back for a few moments enjoying what we had, a friendship that would never end. I kept thinking about all we had done over the years and how it seemed that we had been friends forever.

Our trip was in three days, We had thought of this as a way of kicking off our summer vacation. Neither of us had ever done anything like this, and we felt we may never get another chance to see the world that exists outside the one we live everyday. “Josh, you have towing service for your car right, so why don’t we have them map out the easiest route for us and then tomorrow we can get in some pool time. What do you think?" I stated to him. "I like your thinking, it's actually a great idea. Let's do it. We can pick up the map in the afternoon after we play pool." Josh replied. I figured if I was to join the league that I'd need all the practice I could get even though the chances of beating Josh were slim I still had a big challenge ahead of me. Few people have ever beaten Josh at pool and those that succeeded, lost every rematch ever played. The best way to practice was to play against someone who could pose an incredible challenge and would play to win every time. Josh, was that person he always played to win and I knew that was the challenge I needed to perfect my skills.

Josh looked over at the desk beside him and noticed my book I was working on right where he had left it earlier. "Do you mind if I finish reading what you got so far? I really enjoyed what I had read so far." Josh asked. "It's okay by me, but don't expect too much I'm still having trouble with the last four chapters. I don't think I can come up with a good ending." I replied. Josh appeared to lose himself in my writing and I sat there nervously waiting for his reaction, thoughts of him not liking it went through my head. I had never attempted anything like this before, Josh convinced me months ago to try. He said I need to find my place and that I should take this chance. I reluctantly decided to try and up until now didn't know if I could hold a readers attention long enough. Josh finished reading and looked up with a smile on his face, I didn't know what to think the moment of truth finally arrived. "Well, What do you think? It's okay, you can tell me the truth, I myself don't think it's that good." I told him. "Jim, I was right about your gift. The story is great; you owe it to yourself to finish the book. No one said it would be easy, but you must finish it. When it's done I'll read the rest. If you'll let me and I'll even pay for you to get it copyrighted." Josh answered. Sometimes in a persons life one feels they themselves are never good enough to succeed, but there's always someone close by that can give words of encouragement our friendship was based strongly on those words.

We were both tired from such a long night but neither of us wanted the night to end too soon. The party was one that I would not forget, It's not that often all our friends can get together and hang out with each other. Over the years, most of them got jobs and some moved farther away, but every once in a while we would find the time to see them. Friendship's change but they never fade away they only grow stronger over times that bring new path's for each of us to follow. Josh and I have been lucky enough to live close by, maybe that's one reason why we are always together. "You don't need to pay for my work, I still don't know If I'll be able to finish it. I just want to finish one thing in my life. Every time I start something I can never finish I usually give up when it gets to difficult." I said to him sadly. "That's why it's so important that you take your time. You don't need to rush a masterpiece like this, it will happen if you believe in it. You can actually make a good living as a writer, just open your eyes to the possibilities that are out there. Life's an open road, No one knows what path to take until they reach that fork in the road." Josh explained. "It's just that somedays I feel like I can do anything and other days

I feel like I'll never get anywhere in my life. I get really depressed and feel like maybe I'm just wasting my time trying to be a writer. I wish I knew for sure that I am doing the right thing." I said sadly. "That's the beauty of life, our future isn't written. Life is what we make of it, only we can decide what we do with our life. When you feel that way, just put it aside for awhile and relax, try to have a little fun. Believe me when I tell you, your not wasting your time if you believe in what you're doing." Josh explained to me.

Often enough it felt like things were so clear to me, I did believe in what I was doing but at the same time I always questioned if it was right, maybe I did try to hard when I should've just opened myself up to everything that was around me. " Josh, do you ever get depressed? I mean how do you make it day to day without things getting to you?" I asked him. "Sure, things get to me but I try not to dwell on them. I live for the day and don't worry about tomorrow until it gets here." Josh told me. What Josh said was right, ever since I can remember he always lived his life the way he wanted. Growing up, he always did what he set out to do If he wanted to go out he found a way even if his parents forbid him to. Josh usually had to do things behind his parent's back, but he never got caught. Until recently, his parents became more strict which added more pressure for Josh to deal with. Josh was right about a lot of things but I knew he was hiding his own problems from me. Josh never liked to talk about his personal problems that often because he always put others before him. Josh liked to help others which made me wonder why becoming a doctor was not what he wanted. I watched as Josh fell asleep and I stayed awake thinking about how my life may not be as bad as I thought. I always wanted to be good at something, even find out what my purpose was in life. I couldn't help the way I felt sometimes, maybe that was normal. Life isn't supposed to be easy, it's so full of everyday challenges and to be able to have a friend around to help face them that's what makes life worth fighting for.

I decided to do some more writing, but realized Josh fell asleep on it. I tried not to wake him as I retrieved it from his hand. Life meant so much to me today that I was inspired to continue to write I realized it wouldn't be easy every day, but I was willing to take the time needed to finish what I set out to do. Sitting at the desk, I reread what I had written and was happy with what I had done so far. I turned on the computer and the noise startled Josh out of his sleep. I looked down and saw him look up at me and smile, no words just his expression made me realize he was glad to see I wasn't giving up. He closed his eyes and turned on his side, and I turned my attention back to the screen in front of me. The words started to flow out of me like running water; I couldn't believe my own eyes. At that point everything seemed to fall in to place, I felt lost again in my writing just as I did when I played pool that night. It had been several days since I was able to write as much as I was doing now. I looked at Josh as he slept and felt as though he too knew my thoughts.

The hour passed quickly as I was writing and I found myself becoming very tired, so I saved the work and proceeded to shut down the computer. I quietly stepped over Josh and put the disk in my draw and made my way to my bed. By the time I finally got in bed it was two a.m. and as I lay back, I saw Josh sit up. "I knew you could do it, all you had to do was relax." Josh said as he turned to lay back down. "I thought you were asleep? I didn't mean to wake you if I did." I said quietly. " You didn't wake me, I was just relaxing before I fell asleep. Did you get a lot of writing done?" he asked. "Yeah, I did. I finished another chapter." I said as I sat up in bed. Josh put his arms over his head to stretch and he rolled over on his side and fell asleep. I sat there in bed thinking about our trip, I looked forward to this for along time and couldn't believe how close it was before we left. I couldn't fall right to sleep so I just lay there with my eyes closed and my thoughts running wild in my head. I often thought better at night; it seemed like the perfect time to free my mind of all my pressure.

I lay there in bed thinking of all I had done with Josh over the years, we've had so many adventures that the trip we were about to embark on made me realize how great this summer was turning out. I've always wanted to experience life on the open road as well as see what's out there. A person can find inspiration anywhere as long as they keep their eyes and ears open to what's around them. My inspiration came from many things, such as friends that I never imagined I had. I no longer felt alone, I felt as though I lived an entire lifetime in a single night. Everything was so perfect, seeing everyone I hadn't seen made the night worth more than anyone could ever imagine. Life is worth more when you can spend it with great friends.

The next morning, I awoke early and of course Josh was still sound asleep; he was normally a late sleeper where I was always up early. I got up quietly and headed downstairs to get something to eat. I decided to let Josh sleep in, there was no real need to wake him because he wasn't the easiest person to wake up. I remember the last time he slept over, I got up early and he didn't get up until nearly noon. Evan then, he wasn't ready to get up Josh always liked to sleep late whenever he could. Josh said he'd rather sleep late than listen to his parents argue with him about school. As I headed towards the door, Josh suddenly woke up as if he was startled out of his sound sleep. "What's wrong, Josh? What did you have a nightmare?" I asked him as I stopped. Catching his breath, " Yeah, something like that. I dreamed I was dead and no one was at my funeral." Josh said. "That's kind of weird don't you think? Even if you were dead, Your one of the most popular kid's in school. I doubt you'd be all alone." I said to him. Josh sat up with sweat dripping off him, he had fear in his eyes and I knew it was the worst dream he'd ever had. Josh had told me on more than one occasion, that he has had several dreams similar to the one he had. Josh's nightmares seemed to be getting worse and neither of us knew what they meant. "Maybe you should talk to someone about these dreams of yours. I really don't think this is normal." I explained to him. "I'll be fine, just give me a minute to relax. Is it alright if I use your shower, I don't want anyone to see me like this." Josh asked politely. "Yeah, no problem you know where everything is so help yourself. I'll be downstairs; when your done come on down and we'll go out for breakfeast." I said to him as I headed to the door. Josh got up as I left and headed across the hall to the bathroom. I went downstairs and into the kitchen where my mother was having coffee. “Did you have a nice night? I heard you had a party.” She said smiling. “So, you were in on it too. I didn’t realize what was going on until we got inside.” I said pouring a cup of coffee. “Josh had been planning that for weeks. He told me not to say anything to you.” She said sipping her coffee. “Why am I not surprised. I guess I can’t leave you two alone anymore can I?” I said as I put my cup down on the table. “I had a great night, everyone showed up, even Mike. He played a few of his new songs and forced me on stage.” I said embarrassed. “ I knew they’d all be there. Josh said he was going to tell everyone to show up. By the way, where is Josh.” She said as she noticed he hadn’t come down. “Well, he decided to take a shower, he’ll be down soon. I think we are going out for breakfeast.” I said to her as I finished my coffee.

Josh had finished his shower, and came downstairs to join us at the table. “Thanks for the use of the shower, I really needed that. Do you still want to go for breakfeast?” Josh said. I sat there for a moment, thinking about what had happened earlier that morning. “No problem. Yeah I still want to go. Do you want to drive or should I?” I asked him. I knew Josh might not be up to driving so I figured I would offer to drive so he could relax. “I’ll drive. Besides, after we still have to get the maps for our trip.” Josh stated. “Well, let’s get going then. We’ve got a lot to do before our trip.” I said to him. “Thanks for letting me stay over. I’ll see you before we leave.” Josh said to my mother as we started to the door. I walked quietly to the door, still thinking about what happened that morning unsure of how to help him. I couldn’t always find the right words to talk to people and that often made things difficult. As we got into the car, I realized that my life wasn’t so bad. I had more than I ever imagined and knew that I should be grateful for what I had. Josh didn’t have the freedom I had and I knew that bothered him, things had changed for him over the past few years and I never saw it until this morning at it’s worst. I guess I was to busy with my own life that I never noticed my friends life changing before me. I looked over at him as we got into the car, his eyes revealed more to me than he may ever have intended. “Are you sure you’re okay? If you really want to talk about it, I’ll listen.” I asked him. “Look, I know you want to help, but There’s nothing anyone can really do. If I change my mind I’ll let you know I promise.” He said to me.

We backed out of the driveway and I still felt so helpless, as though we were distant from each other. I knew I couldn't push the issue, but I still wished he talked to me. We headed for our usual donut shop, which was not to far from my house. The morning air was clear and many people were just stepping outside to get their morning paper. I always watched people everywhere we went, I guess it made me feel like I knew everyone and was a part of their lives. Josh put the radio on and turned up the volume, his favorite song was on and he seemed to relax as he listened and tried without success to sing along. I laughed to myself only because he knew what I would say. I looked over and saw him crack a smile, I knew he felt better hearing a song that he actually knew well. "What? I may not sing well, but no one's perfect." He said as we turned the corner. "I didn't say a word, Besides the singer must be perfect, at least he can sing!" I said laughing. "Some friend you are, I thought you were on my side." He asked. "I am, but you couldn't sing to save your life. At least he can keep a tune, you can't even keep up the beat tapping your fingers on the wheel." I said trying not to laugh. We pulled into the donut shop, and Josh turned down the radio so we could order. "Welcome, may I take your order?" the voice asked politely. " Yeah, two coffees, black with two sugars and half dozen donuts, chocolate frosted." Josh replied to the intercom. "That will be six fifty, please pull forward." The voice answered. Josh drove up to the window and I handed him a ten, It was in fact my turn to buy. After we got our breakfeast, Josh drove to the parking lot and we ate there.

Josh was silent for the longest time which made me wonder if things were all right or if he just wanted me to think that it was. "Josh, your pretty quiet, is everything alright?" I asked him. "Yeah, everything's cool. I was just thinking about our trip. I'll pick you up early so be ready. I want to get an early start so we can avoid traffic." He said to me. I couldn't believe Josh lied to me, I knew something was bothering him and he just sat there and lied to me. I figured I might as well drop it, he'd talk to me if he wanted and I can't force him to tell me about what's bothering him if he doesn't want to.We finished our coffee and pulled out of the donut shop, we had a lot to do before out trip. "Do we still have time to play pool, or would you rather skip it and get our maps?" I asked him as we drove away. "I think we should skip it, we can play pool at the hotel. We should get our maps and then pack our gear so we'll be all set for tomorrow.

There's plenty of time for pool." Josh replied. I was disappointed, but I knew we did have a lot to do and the day wasn't passing so slow either. We drove towards the map center and listened to the radio as we drove. Some things just never change.

The drive itself was not a long one; we made it in fifteen minutes and pulled into the parking lot. "Do you have your membership card?" I asked Josh as he parked. "Yeah, I do. You coming in or do you want to stay out here?" Josh said as he got out of the car. "I'm coming, I just had to clean my glasses." I told him. Once we got inside, we found our way to the main desk. The lady behind the counter took Josh's card and went to the file to get our maps for us. She returned and showed us the path they marked out for us. The path seemed easy enough; Josh was the best with directions he understood maps better than anyone I ever knew. "Okay, let's go. I'll drop you off and then I'll go home and get my stuff together. I should be at your house early so make sure your ready." Josh said as we left the map center. I looked at my watch and it was a little after three in the afternoon, I figured I could pack and maybe go out for alittle while with my other friend.

We got to the car and Josh continued to study the route they mapped out, he seemed to be memorizing it like it was nothing more than a bunch of lines. I got in and Josh folded the map and put it over the visor so he wouldn't lose it. "I guess you won't need that. What did you do, memorize the map already?" I asked him. He turned to me and just smiled as he started the car. As we backed out, I thought about everything we did together and how this trip was going to be the biggest thing we ever did. We drove back to my house without saying a word, both of us thinking about the days ahead. As we pulled into my driveway, Josh turned to me and started to say something. "Remember, I'll be here early so be ready. Tomorrows our day, everything changes and our lives will be different." Josh said to me. I noticed a tear in his eye as he turned away, as if trying to hide it from me. I got out of the car and headed in side, still wondering what Josh meant exactly. "That you Jim, You're home early is everything alright." My mom asked. "Yeah, everything's fine. Were already for tomorrow, he'll be here early to get me." I said leaning against the front door. "Did you pack yet, or are you going to do that tonight." She asked. "I think I'll go out with Jeremy for alittle while tonight, if that's all right." I asked her as I gathered my senses. "Sure, just be careful. Do you plan on being out late, if so I'll leave the light on and remember to take your key." She asked me. I walked into the kitchen and saw her as she cleaned the dishes; I realized how lucky I was to have a mother that cared enough to give me my space. "I might be out a little late, but I'll let you know when I'm home. Thanks." I said to her. She put the dishtowel down and sat at the table to have her drink. "Thanks for what?" She asked as she sipped her drink. "For just being you and not pushing me." I replied. My parents never interfered with my life, but I knew they'd be there if I ever needed them.

I went upstairs to call Jeremy and see if he wanted to hang out at the beach and do some rollerblading and maybe get something to eat. Jeremy was another person I could talk to, we met at school and he taught me to skate. As I looked for his number, the phone rang and I picked it up quickly so not to disturb my mother's work. "Hello, is Jim there?" the voice said. "Speaking, is that you Jeremy, I was just about to call you and see what you were doing." I asked. "Well what a coincidence, I was hoping we could do something before you left for your trip. You got anything in mind?" Jeremy asked. "How about rollerblading, I thought we could go down to the beach along the boardwalk? Unless you have something else in mind?" I asked him. "No, actually that sounds great I'll meet you there in a half hour." Jeremy said. "I'll be there, maybe we can grab a bite to eat I haven't eaten yet." I told him. "Sounds like a plan to me, I'll see you there. Bye" Jeremy answered. I hung up the phone and searched frantically for my blades, I knew I left them in my room somewhere but I couldn't remember exactly where. I opened the closest door and got a lucky break, right in front of me on the floor I found them. I grabbed my backpack and headed downstairs to tell my mother I was going balding with Jeremy for a while.

Once downstairs, I went into the kitchen and grabbed a soda and put my sneakers in my backpack. "You going out again? Don't forget to pack for the trip." My mother asked from the living room. I walked into the living room and sat down. "Yeah, Jeremy called me and wanted to go blading before I leave. I was going to call him but I guess he read my mind. I won't be out too late." I told her as I put my skates on. "Let me know when you come in tonight, okay" she said. I got up out of the chair and picked up my backpack and headed to the door. I still needed a lot of practice blading, not to mention that it was quite relaxing. I started toward the beach and found myself a little out of practice. The sun started to go down and the air was still very warm I wasn't the only one blading half the neighborhood kids were outside enjoying the night. Some kids set up ramps to jump, while still others just skated around with their friends. Skating had become a popular way of transportation lately as well as great exercise. So many people could skate so well and I was only a beginner, I had only been skating for a couple of months. Jeremy on the other hand, had been skating most of his life. I loved the feeling of rolling down the road with the cool air in my face.

Once I reached the beach, I realized I was going too fast and couldn't stop very well. I saw Jeremy in the distance and he spotted me to late, I was heading straight towards him unable to stop. Jeremy jumped out of the way in time and I skated right onto the grass and landed face first on the lawn. I lay there for a moment before turning on my back and looked up as Jeremy stood above me. "Still have trouble stopping? I guess we'll have to work on that later." Jeremy said as he reached out his hand to help me up. "Thanks. I was preoccupied and forgot where I was. I definitely need to concentrate on what I'm doing." I said moaning. Jeremy skated around me and stopped like it was nothing. He liked to show off his skating ability. "You really enjoy rubbing it in don't you?" I said to him. "Sorry, You'll catch on its not that hard. So, what's up with you? Tomorrows your trip, are you excited?" Jeremy asked. "Yeah, I can't wait. But that's tomorrow, let's skate." I told Jeremy. I waited as Jeremy put his skates on, he always drives to the beach mainly because he has a new car and likes to show it off.

Skating almost proved to be an opportunity of a lifetime for Jeremy, he entered a contest which consisted of fifty of the top skaters and came in second. The first prize was a chance to skate for a professional stunt team. Second place had its rewards also, ten thousand dollars which he used to get his car. Jeremy wasted no time buying the car he'd always wanted. "You ready, or do you still want to day dream? How long you plan on staying, I know your leaving early so I don't think we should skate too late." Jeremy stated as he finished tying his skate. "I wasn't daydreaming. I'll stay for a couple of hours or so, I'm still too excited to sleep." I replied. "Let's do it!" Jeremy shouted as he skated away. I caught up to him quicker than I thought I would. Jeremy knew skating like the back of his hand; he never missed a turn or a perfect jump.

We skated along the boardwalk slowly because it was still a little crowded. Jeremy skated between people walking without coming close to bumping into anyone. As for me, I was still relatively an amateur and skated more slowly than he did. The wind blew the water mist across the boardwalk spraying us as we skated. The cool water felt great against my face as I zigzagged between people myself with more confidence. I could see Jeremy in the distance showing off as usual. I managed to slow down, which was actually a first, and Jeremy spotted me and came over too. "What's up, you don't seem like you're really into it tonight? Is something wrong?" Jeremy asked concerned. I stood there looking at him wondering if I should even tell him about Josh; considering the fact that we came to skate not discuss our problems. I really wanted to skate, but I couldn't stop thinking about Josh's attitude later that day. I knew inside something was wrong but I couldn't get him to talk. I sat down on the bench and Jeremy joined me sitting beside me sipping his water. "It's not you, I'm worried about Josh, he wasn't acting right this afternoon." I said to him as I took a drink from his water bottle. "I didn't mean to ruin the night." I said. "It's no problem. What's wrong with Josh?" he said. "I'm not quite sure, I get the feeling something's really wrong. He won't even talk too me and I feel helpless." I replied folding my hands. "Hey, it's cool, when he's ready to talk, you'll be the first one he comes to you know that. The two of you have been friends for so long, he wouldn't keep secrets from you." Jeremy reassured me. "I know, but this is different. He seems closed off from everything lately. I only wish he'd talk to me or someone at least." I stated. I stood up and skated to the railing, leaning against it and looking at the waves roll onto the beach. I could feel the power of each wave as it rolled towards the beach. Many a times I wished that I had that power.

Jeremy stood up as well and skated towards me, "Let it go, when he's ready he'll tell you, I know he will." I realized he was right, I could do nothing until Josh was ready, and only he knew when the time would be. "I wish I had my camera, this is such a great shot. It must be so cool to be able to swim out there." I said. "Yeah, but you'll get your chance one day, When you break your fear." Jeremy replied. "Think so? Do you think I'll learn to swim one day?" I asked him. "All you need is to trust someone to teach you, hell, I'll teach you if you want." Jeremy replied. "I appreciate the offer, but I'm not ready yet I guess. I need more time." I answered. "Maybe that's how

Josh feel's, understand what I mean?" Said Jeremy. I thought for a moment, and realized that he made a lot of sense. I had to realize I couldn't solve everyone's problems, I could only be there to listen when I was needed.

I stood there amazed at the sight before me, the water so calm and peaceful the sun setting, it was the perfect picture. We both stood there and watched as the sun disappeared slowly into the horizon, until the darkness filled the remaining light. It was a memory that burned into your thoughts, one a person wished would never fade away. The people at the beach slowly packed up there belongings, leaving only those who lived for the night. The air itself never changed it remained warm, unusual for the night. It was the perfect time for skating, no one around to get in the way and the air was just right. As the remaining crowd of people left, we watched the waves rolling onto the shore. I saw for the first time waves that towered over me, as powerful as they came crashing down they disappeared into the night. The smell of the ocean seemed to fill the night air, and the moon being full lit up the beach. The night was perfect, so relaxing that a person would forget all that bothers him. I watched as Jeremy skated along the path wishing I had brought Josh along, even just so he could see the atmosphere before us. Jeremy skated like the professional he was, never missing an opportunity in which to show off his skills.

I remained mesmerized by what was before me; I couldn't help but lose myself in the night. There was always something about the night that made me feel like I belonged to it. It was as if the night swallowed me up and left no trace of my existence for anyone to discover. I felt as much a part of the night as I took a deep breath and realized how peaceful it was. Often I wondered how people could overlook the beauty that the night had to offer for those willing to let it take them. "Hey Jim! I thought we came to skate? Quit daydreaming and let's skate." Jeremy shouted from a distance. I snapped out of my daze and sped off in the direction he yelled. "Sorry, I guess I got caught up in the moment. I still can't believe how great it is here at night." I said as I skated up to him. "There's nothing to be sorry about. Let's just skate and leave everything else behind for one night. Besides, it might be some time before we can do this again." Jeremy replied as he raced off. I followed him as best I could unable to keep up. We skated for what seemed hours, the time just passed and I decided I should be getting back soon.

We made our way back the way we came, which seemed longer than before. When we reached Jeremy's car, I slowed down so I would not hit his car; a prize like this deserved all the caution one could muster up. Jeremy, who wasn't far behind saw me and smiled, I had finally conquered how to stop. I hadn't practiced skating until tonight and I guess sometimes one can accomplish anything once they set their mind to it. "Congratulations, you finally did it. I told you if you had to do it that you would be able to stop. Not to mention, If you did hit my car I'd have to kick your ass." Jeremy said to me smiling. Jeremy got his keys out and opened the driver's side door. I stood up against the side as Jeremy sat down in the seat and removed his skates. He sat there and just stared into the night for a moment. "What's up with you? You never bug out, is something wrong?" I asked him. "Not at all. I was just thinking that we should do this more often. It's been awhile since we've done anything and I kind of missed it. Do you want to skate when you get back from your trip?" Jeremy asked disappointed as though I forgot about our friendship. "You know I like to skate, it's just that I've been very busy lately." I said removing my skates for awhile. "Well, it's like you're never around. If your too busy then just say so, I thought we were friends." Jeremy said. "We are. I've been busy writing, or at least trying to write. I didn't mean to ignore you, It's just that sometimes I get so wrapped up in my writing that I forget about everything around me. I never meant to forget about anyone." I answered. "Yeah, I know. I know how you get, and sometimes I get that way myself with my skating. How's the writing going anyway?" Jeremy replied. "It's going alright, except I think I got writers block. I can't seem to get past the last paragraph I'm working on." I answered. "Well, maybe the trip might help with that. I hear the both of you have been planning it for sometime, I'm sure it'll be great. Besides, I'm sure we'll skate when you get back." Jeremy stated excitedly. We sat there for a moment collecting our thoughts not even thinking about the time. I was always one, who enjoyed talking, especially if it meant learning more about a friend than I did. I looked at my watch and realized it was getting late. "Jeremy, I do want to skate when I get back so make sure you call me in a week. I'm sure we'll have a lot to catch up on." I said putting on my skates. "Do you want a ride, I could drop you off so you don't get yourself killed. I like having someone to skate with and I'd feel bad if you got hit by a car." Jeremy asked me. "Yeah, that sounds like a great idea. Skating in daylight is easier than at night. You sure you don't mind?" I asked him. "No sweat, Get in." Jeremy said reaching over to unlock the door. Jeremy knew I wasn't as good a skater as he, and I did appreciate the company as well as the offer. "Thanks a lot. Are you sure it's not to far out of the way for you?" I asked. "Don't worry about it, I think it would be safer anyway." Jeremy said starting the car. I sat back and removed my skates so I wouldn't scratch up his rugs.

We pulled out of the beach parking lot and headed back to my house, I knew this was out of his way, Jeremy lived on the other side of town and it would take him at least another hour before he got home himself. I sat silent for a time as we drove to my house just thinking about the trip tomorrow. Jeremy turned up the radio a bit and they played a song I knew very well, it happened to be Mike's new song off his recent album. It felt great to hear his music finally being played on the radio. "Isn't that Mike's new song?" Jeremy asked excitedly. I reached over to turn it up a little louder. "Yeah, he did it, he finally got on the radio. This is so great, his records are sure to sell big time now." I answered. I couldn't believe my ears; Mike had been waiting for this to happen for a long time. Mike was on his way to getting his name known for sure now and I could only imagine how he must have felt at that time. I was so glad that things were looking up for him. I only wished I could have the same luck as he did. Often I thought that I'd never finish my book and that I was wasting my time on a dream that would never happen. Maybe it just wasn't my time yet maybe I had more to do before my dreams came true. "Dreams do come true." Was what Josh always said to me, those words forever rang in my ears and I had to believe that one day it would be my turn to make it in the real world.

We pulled into my driveway and Jeremy put the car in park, I sat there quiet for a moment. "What's up, aren't you happy for Mike?" Jeremy asked. "Of course, I just hope I get that kind of luck one day. Sometimes I feel I'm wasting my time. I feel like it's not worth the effort anymore to try to write a book." I answered. "For what it's worth, Keep trying one day it will be your turn. If you give up you'll never know what you could have had." Jeremy said. I knew he was right but it was never easy to push aside bad my fears of failure at the drop of a match. We sat and talked for a short time before we realized the time, Jeremy had a long enough drive ahead of him and me, I still had some packing to do. “Well, I should be going, I’ll see you when you get back. Have fun.” Jeremy said to me shaking my hand. “I will. I’ll call you when I get back and thanks for letting me skate with you.” I said as I got out of the car. I carried my skates, because I was too lazy and too tired to put my sneakers on. I turned and saw Jeremy pull away and it felt as though the things around me even the people were changing and leaving me.

For that one instant, I felt alone. I felt as though I was the only one in the world around me. That feeling scared me, and I couldn’t shake it even as I opened the door to my house and went in. I crept up the stairs quietly, I knew it was very late and didn’t want to wake my mother, nor did I want her to know I was somewhat later than I planned on being. I walked into my room and turned on the light, It was then I noticed the note on my desk, I picked it up and opened it. *Busted, You’re caught. I’m not mad, just kidding. Hope you had a great night and by the way have a great trip tomorrow I’ll see you when you get back. Love Mom.* I stood there and laughed to myself, I could never pull anything over her, and she always managed to catch me. I put my skates next to my bed; I sat down and felt so incredibly tired. I just sat there collecting my thoughts before I made any effort to finish packing. I picked up my book I was working on and stared at it and cried to myself silently. I felt so scared that I’d never finish it, that I’d never know what it was like to be known. I decided I was too tired to finish packing, I figured I could finish in the morning before Josh arrived, he never was that early for anything. I just laid back on the bed, too tired to even change for bed and I just drifted off to sleep thinking about my friends as well as the trip ahead of me.

CHAPTER 3

The morning came fast that day; it was to be our greatest time and our last chance at freedom before our senior year. Josh and I had planned for this trip for weeks. We planned on traveling to New Hampshire and seeing the sites. We also wanted time to see what the future had for us. Josh was more intelligent than he let on; he scored highly on his S.A.T test in school, which opened up a wide variety of options for him. Josh never wanted to be treated any differently because of his scores. Josh and I had been through a lot together, after all we had been friends for over twelve years, not many people could say they had a friendship that was as tight as ours was. We knew everything about each other; there were no secrets.

Saturday finally arrived and I was still tired after the night before, Josh was due to arrive within an hour which gave me plenty of time to get the rest of my gear ready, or so I thought. I heard a car door slam outside and couldn't believe my eyes as I looked out the window, Josh was actually early. "Jim, Are you ready yet or what?" yelled Josh as he looked up at me. I opened the window and yelled down to him. "Do you have any idea what time it is, You're early." I didn't expect him to show up at 5 A.M. I thought I'd have more time to get ready. "I want to get an early start, you know to beat the traffic. We'll make better time if we leave early." Josh yelled. "Quiet, you'll wake up the neighborhood then we'll really be in trouble. Just wait downstairs, I'll be right down." I said throwing him my house key. I closed the window as Josh made his way to the door to unlock it and come in. I gathered what gear I had already packed and hoped I had everything that I needed. I made my way down the stairs carrying all three of my bags, but I neglected to notice the spare skate on the stairs. "Look out you fool," Josh said just as I stepped on it and fell on my ass. My bags flew high in the air and came down on me to make my trip more painful. Without thinking twice, Josh reached out his hand to help me up off the stairs; I never had to worry about falling because I always knew Josh would be there when I needed him.

"Are you okay?" he asked as he pulled me to my feet. "I'm fine, thanks. Now I remember where I left my spare skate, hell of a way to find them." I said laughing. I bent down to pick up my bags and noticed to bandage on Josh's wrist. "What happened to your wrist?" I asked him as he tried to hide it from me. "Nothing, minor flesh wound the cat clawed me this morning." Josh replied as if really trying to hide something. Josh and I always told each other the truth and this I didn't believe was the truth. As he helped me with my bags he put his hand on my shoulder and said, " Don't worry, it's nothing serious." I left a note for my mother and we closed the door behind us as we headed to the car. "Open the trunk, I'll put my stuff inside. " I asked him. Josh opened the car door and flipped the switch inside to open the trunk. I quickly put my gear inside and still thought I had forgotten something as I closed the trunk. As I got in the car, he asked, "So put some sounds in and let's rock." I rummaged through his so called organized tape case to find something appropriate to listen to and found the right tape and put it in. I knew then and there that this was going to be a trip neither of us would ever forget.

Josh put the car in gear and we were finally on our way, we drove for miles just listening to the music. "Did you remember your notebook so you can log our trip, it might make for a great new book someday." He asked as he turned the radio down. "Of course I did, You'd never let me forget anyway." I replied to him pulling it out of my backpack. I never understood why it was so important that I log our trip until later. "So are you ready for senior year, or what?" I asked him. "I'm not sure, I mean I'm looking forward to it but I'm nervous too." He replied. "What are you afraid of, it's our last year this is the final road in front of us." I said to him as he drove. " I know, There's so much that can happen between now and then." He said to me. I sat confused at his reply, which made no sense to me. "At least you got everything set for your future." I said trying to reassure him. "Is that what you think, that everything will be fine because I'm registered for college already?" Josh snapped at me. "What's wrong, I thought you'd be glad about your acceptance to college." I stated in return. "I am, I'm sorry for snapping at you, It's just that I really don't want to talk about college. I just want to relax and enjoy our trip. Don't you realize we won't see each other as often when I leave for college, I just don't want to think about that." Josh answered sadly. "You have to do what's right for you, not us. This is a chance of a lifetime you can't pass this up." I said to him.

As we drove I felt, as though my bladder was going to explode, I couldn't wait any longer. "Hey, let's pull over. I need to use the rest room." I asked him. "You got one hell of a bladder problem." Josh said laughing. "Well we could use gas as well so it's not like it'll be a waste of time. Besides I think it's your driving that makes me so nervous." I said jokingly. We trusted each other enough that we could insult each other, maybe that's one thing that made our friendship so strong. I gave Josh ten dollars as we pulled up to the pump, and I opened the door and ran to the bathroom. "Hey! Close the dam door at least." Josh yelled as I ran. "Sorry, I really have to go bad." I yelled back. Josh got out of the car and filled up the gas tank and paid the attendant. "Do you have a water hose near the bathroom?" he asked the attendant. "Yeah, why?" the attendant asked. Josh went over and picked up the hose and turned it on and pinched the hose so it wouldn't leak until the last moment. I cleaned my glasses while inside; the dust of the open road sure does a number on them. I opened the door and got the biggest shock of my life, Josh sprayed me with the hose soaking me to the skin. "Turn it off!" I yelled as he continued to spray me. "What the hell." I said dripping wet. Josh stood there laughing his head off; at least one of us thought it was funny. "I told you I'd get even for that wise crack about my driving. Looks like you may have to walk the rest of the way, your not riding in my car soaked." Josh laughed outloud. "Oh, and you were the one that soaked me, and I have to walk?" I said to him still dripping wet. I couldn't believe Josh had the guts to pull a stunt like this. I guess I shouldn't have underestimated him. "Don't just stand there, go get my bag from the trunk so I can change my clothes, or I will ride in the car soaked." I said to him. Laughing and pointing Josh headed towards the car to get my bag, and as he turned his back I myself couldn't resist the hose before me and picked it up and nailed him directly in the back of the head.

After I changed my clothes, we drove for what seemed an eternity and we laughed all the way. It felt great to be young and free, just two friends sharing a great trip. We arrived on a small town and decided to stop for the night, Josh had been driving for at least four hours and began to tire. We had two weeks for our vacation, which gave us plenty of time to travel and enjoy the time, and laughs we had so far. The hotel we chose had an indoor pool and Josh, who always enjoyed the water, was thrilled, decided to go down to the pool after we unpacked. Our room was on the third floor, which had a great view of the town outside. After we finished unpacking, Josh went into the bathroom and put on his bathing suit and headed down to the pool. I stayed behind and wrote of our great water hose fight. It's funny how something incredibly dumb made us laugh, I don't think I'll ever forget that water fight. Two hours later, he returned and asked why I didn't come with him. "Don't tell me you forgot that I can't swim? It's not really worth going in if I can't swim." I said to him. "I'll teach you if you want, it's not that hard and you know you can trust me." Josh replied putting his shirt on. "It's not that I don't trust you, it's just that I'm afraid." I answered. "What are you afraid of? It's only a pool and it's not too deep. I won't let you drown, and besides you could just sit on the pool stairs and relax." Josh said. "It's just not that simple, I want to learn, but I'm afraid that I will drown." I answered. "When you're ready, ask and I'll teach you to swim, I will not make fun of you or let you drown. I wish you'd trust me enough to let me prove it to you." Josh said as he sat on the bed. I knew that Josh meant well, which is probably why we had been friends for so many years and been there for each other in any crisis.

Josh went to finish changing and I ordered room service, since neither of us had eaten since we left that morning. I sat there thinking how lucky he was to know how to swim and how much I wish I could swim as well. I remembered one time we were at the lake, I watched him as he swam the entire width of the lake like he belonged there. I wished I were able to be out there with him enjoying the water the way it was always meant to be. Sometimes I felt that not knowing how to swim caused me to lose out on a lot of great nights swimming. Twenty minutes later, dinner arrived which consisted of hamburgers and fries, a teenager's favorite food. Josh came out of the bathroom, wearing his shorts and a tee shirt ready to eat. Josh was never one for dressing for dinner, I remember at Christmas one year he wore his boxer shorts and a tee shirt to dinner, all he said was " Hey, they can be worn as shorts too." Josh was one of a kind; he always believed one should be comfortable and never worry about what others thought. If we all worried about what they thought, then life wouldn't be so interesting. I guess he was right. As the night wore on, we listened to our tapes and relaxed. Its was so great not being told when to go to bed, when to eat, what to eat, and even how long we could be out for. We both looked forward to the day when college came; we even planned on being roommates in our own apartment. The freedom we had that night was what every teen dreamed of, we finally lived that dream. It felt like we were on top of the world that night, so much freedom that we decided what was best for us, even if it was for only two weeks. "Do you want to play cards?" Josh asked as he reached inside his bag for the deck. "Sure, what do you always carry a deck of cards with you?" I asked him putting down my notebook. "Name the game." Josh said as he shuffled the deck. "How about twenty one? It's my best game." I answered. Josh agreed and began to deal the cards, avoiding eye contact for some particular reason. It felt as though he was trying to hide something from me.

I picked up my hand and arranged my cards, and asked him straight out what I had been wanting to all day. "What's bothering you Josh, It's like you're not yourself lately?" He looked up at me finally, from behind his cards and I could see a single tear in his eye as it rolled down his cheek. "I'm scared." He sobbed. I'd never seen him cry in all the time I've known him that scared me. "What are you scared of?" I asked him as I put my cards down. "I can't handle the pressure my parents are putting on me to become a doctor, I can't do it." Josh said wiping his eyes. "I thought you wanted to be a doctor, it's all you have ever talked about. Why didn't you tell me this before?" I asked him. Josh stood up from the floor and sat on the bed across from me. "It's my parent's that want me to be a doctor, they expect me to follow in my grandfathers footsteps. They never asked me what I wanted to do." Josh sobbed. "Did you talk to your parents about this? Why don't you tell them how you feel, It's your life and your decision as to what you do in the future." I replied. From that moment on, everything I thought I knew about his parents changed, how could I ever see them the way I did before. I never knew his parents were that determined to decide his future for him. I knew it was wrong, but Josh's parents may not have known what it was doing to their son on the inside. "They won't listen to me, they insist on deciding what I do. They say it's what I should do." Josh replied. I could see how much this bothered him; I stared him in the eyes and felt his pain. "They even filled out my college registration form, I couldn't even change it." Josh said as he covered his face with his hands. "They expect me to become something I don't want to, I know being a doctor is great but it's not what I want in life. I can't deal with other peoples lives everyday. The responsibility is too much for me." Josh answered. "You have to talk to them again, it's your life no one should be able to tell you how to live it." I told him. "Sometimes, I wish I was never born. I only want to live life a little before I decide what to do, Is that so wrong?" Josh cried. "Don't talk like that, life is what you make of it, don't let your parents decide your life for you. It's up to each of us to make our life something we can be proud of." I stated.

We sat silent for a long time, Josh finally laid back on his bed and me, and I tried to be the friend I could to him by listening to him as he spoke. I never knew he felt that way about life and that scared me. I realized sometimes there are secrets even friends have to keep from each other, but this one was to big for him to handle alone. "Everyone's got a choice in life, we are all free to decide for ourselves what path our lives will take us. You have to talk to your parents; you have to make them listen. Tell them you could never be happy unless you chose which road you follow." I stated. Josh just lay there as if the world had beaten him, before me lay my friend with all his dreams broken and only he could make the next move. "I shouldn't have involved you, it's not your problem. I'm the one who may never be happy in life." Josh said as he walked over to the window and looked into the night.

That night I saw a side of my friend I never knew existed, A part that scared me and made me realize how we were all human after all. We all see ourselves as being happy, but some of us in this world may not be as happy as we think. I always believed Josh wanted to be a doctor, he never told me the truth until tonight and I felt as though I didn't really know him as well as I thought I did. I sat up in my bed, watching him and thinking how he could have kept this from me, without even talking to anyone about it. I wasn't sure if I could help, I only knew I could listen to him and support him the way a friend should. "Thing's will work out Josh, Talk to them again, you can't give up." I said finally. Josh turned away from the window and I saw the pain in his eyes before he uttered a single word, it sent shivers down my spine. "I told you, my parents will not give me a say in what I do. I don't get the choices everyone else gets in life. My life has been decided for me, no one can change their minds, not even you." Josh said with hate in his voice. I saw the fear in his eyes and it was nothing like I thought fear could ever be described as, he had it and it was ripping him apart inside. "I'm going for a walk, I don't want to blow up at you, I realize your only trying to help and I appreciate that but there's nothing that can be done." Josh said as he slipped on his sneakers. Josh stood up and opened the door and walked out closing it behind him. I felt I'd'lost him. Sometimes a friend can only do so much even then it may not be enough to help.

Josh loved to walk at night, often at times we'd walk at night, he said it cleared his head and helped him to think. We had been on many late night walks, sharing laughs, even getting into a little trouble too. One night we went to a place he found the night before, and we had a couple of beers which of course was illegal, but hell everyone's done it at one point in their lives. We talked for hours that night, we even laughed too. It felt great to be taking such a chance, but it was worth the risk. I got so drunk that night I had to stay at Josh's house, I couldn't even walk straight and I only had three, he had six and was still sober. We had a great time that night. I'll never forget all those good times we shared together. An hour passed, I was in bed wondering if he was all right, when the door opened and Josh walked in. He kicked off his shoes and came over to my bed. "I'm really sorry if I snapped at you, I realize you mean well and care. I'm lucky to have a friend I can trust and I apologize." Josh said to me. "I'm here if you need to talk, I only wish I could be of more help to you." I stated concerned. "I'm going to sit up for alittle while then take a shower, I'll see you in the morning. Don't worry about anything I'll be fine." Josh replied to me as he walked over to the table and sat down. I went in to the bathroom to change and went to bed soon after, Josh was still sitting there in deep thought alone. I fell asleep not long after my head hit the pillow, it had been a long day and I was tired, very tired.

I awoke to the alarm, it read seven a.m. and I looked over at Josh's bed, it hadn't been slept in. I got up quickly and heard the shower running I figured he got up earlier and decided to shower in the morning instead of last night. I walked to the door and knocked without getting an answer. "Hey Josh! What are you doing using all the hot water, save some for me." I said as I slowly opened the door. I walked in and stood in shock at what I saw before me. I stood motionless for a time before I reacted at the horror before me. Josh was lying in the bathtub, wearing his boxers and his wrists slit, blood everywhere. I screamed out as I fell to the floor. "No, God why, why." I reached over to him and pulled his lifeless body from the tub. My hands full of blood, as I tried to wake him as though he were still alive. I sat there with him, crying all the time I held him, I never thought for a moment Josh would do this to himself. I laid him down and left the room to call for an ambulance, "911, what's your emergency?" The voice said. "My friend is dead, I think he committed suicide, Please you've got to help." I cried out as I fell to my knees unable to talk anymore. I heard the operator say she would trace the call and that help was on the way. I couldn't bring myself to deal with this; I sat there and cried until the ambulance showed up. The police arrived and went into the bathroom to search and an officer came out a short time later with a piece of paper. "I found this in his shirt pocket, it's addressed to you I guess. As soon as you're done reading it, I'll need to read it as well, It's evidence and we need to verify suicide. I'm very sorry." The officer said handing me the folded note. I got up off the floor, my socks covered in his blood, and still shaking I unfolded the note and began to read.

> Jim,
>
> *"I'm sorry for ruining our trip. I always trusted you and that never changed, my problems were not yours and I don't want you to blame yourself for my acts. You've always been a great friend to me and I'll miss you. I wish things could have been different but I couldn't find any way to tell my parents the truth, I knew they would never listen and things would not have changed. I never would've been happy. I tried to think of another way but failed to find a solution. You were my best friend and I never intended to hurt you like this. One of us will succeed and I know it will be you, so don't give up hope like I did. You will be a great writer someday, never give up that dream. Live for the both of us! In my pants pocket you'll find my necklace, the eagle, I want you to have it. Wear it and I'll always be closeby, perhaps it will help you to keep your head in the clouds like a great writer should be. Thanks for being my friend; I'll never forget you.*
>
> *Josh 1987 summer trip.*

After reading the note, I felt more and more like I had failed him. The officer came back a short time later and asked if He could read the note, promising me that it would be returned to me. I handed it to him unwilling to part with the last thing I had left of him. "In the note, he mentioned he left me his necklace in his pants pocket, could I please go get it? I would really like to get it before something happens to it, he promised it would be mine." I said sobbing. "I think that will be okay, just let us cover up the body, I don't think you should see him like that anymore." The officer replied to me. I grabbed the officer by the shoulder as he turned to walk in to the bathroom, "Wait, I need to remember him the way he is not covered up, he's still my friend. Please just give me a few more minutes with him. I'll get the necklace and I won't touch anything else, I promise. I just need to see him again before you take him away." The officer seemed apprehensive about the suggestion I made, but agreed and cleared everyone out of the room for me. "Thanks, I appreciate it. He was my best friend." I replied to the officer. "If you need anything let me know, I'll be outside the door. Try not to stay to long, it might make things worse for you." The officer said closing the door. I went in and sat down beside his body, they cleaned him up a bit and bandaged his wrists to absorb the rest of the bleeding. I reached over and picked up his pants, and searched his pockets for the necklace. It was in his front pocket, I pulled it out and it fell to the floor like a dying bird falling from the sky. I cried softly to myself, still wondering why I didn't take the time to talk to him more. I thought I could have prevented all of this by just listening more than I had done. I picked up the necklace and held it tight in my hands, clenching it in my fists. I never wanted to let it go. "Josh, why, why couldn't you have just talked to me. I tried to remember all the things we had done, all I could really think about was how I failed him. I'd never been alone before and for the first time, I truly was alone. Josh and I were inseparable, we did everything together from the time we met and now it came to a crashing halt. It literally felt like someone was out to get us, like we had done something wrong all these years and it was time for revenge.

After a while, the door opened up and the officer said I got ten more minutes then they have to move him to the morgue to prepare him for the trip home. I sat there as question after question filled my mind. How could he do this to me? Why did you leave me alone? Did I do something wrong? Could I have prevented all of this? Being alone, was something I was not used to, and couldn't handle at all. My mind seemed to fill with every idea of how I might have been able to stop him, If only I was awake instead of sleeping. It's strange how a person's mind reacts to death; it shows all the mistakes in your life at first. I prayed for the first time in years over my friend's body, I prayed not for him alone, but forgiveness for failing him. I felt so cold inside like I committed the worst crime at that moment. I still had to find the words to tell his parents and his little brother, I didn't now what to say or how to say it. I picked up the necklace and stared at it, remembering when I bought it, we had gone camping in the woods that weekend. It was spring and we wanted to rough it, as we were getting food, I spotted the chain and told him he should get it, he refused to spend the money on it. Josh paid for the food and went out to the car; I bought it for him, because I was like it belonged to him. Its spirit seemed to be like Josh, free and full of life. The wings spread out like it was flying I could almost imagine the eagle flying above the trees like he owned the sky, no one to hold it back and able to see for miles ahead. Josh was sitting in the car when I got out of the store, I held it out and let it dangle in front of him, and he stared at me with fire in them. "Why did you buy that, it cost too much? Besides, I didn't think you like eagles." Josh said as he started the car. "It's not for me, It's for you. I felt it belonged to you, like somehow the two of you are one. I realize it sounds crazy, but it's true. I could almost see it flying when I held it, it was like I was a part of it and I could fly." I stated. Josh reached for it and couldn't take his eyes off it, I knew he wanted it I saw that in his eyes in the store. Josh was never really one for spending money foolishly. So, I did. "Thanks a lot, its pretty cool. I can feel it, I can almost see it fly too." Josh said as he put it on. I wanted days like that to never end, it seemed like we would be friends forever, I guess things change over time. I just never thought something like this would ever happen. I like a lot of people took for granted that life was forever, that nothing would ever separate us. I cried one last time before I left him that day. I felt abandoned and alone. I didn't know how my life would turn out from then on.

Standing outside the hotel, I watched as they loaded my friend into the hearse and closed the door to what seemed like the end of the world. The car drove off; the emptiness of being alone set in like being hit by a truck. The officer put his hand on my shoulder, "I'm really sorry about your friend. If you need anything here's my number, feel free to call anytime." He said as he handed me his card. I hadn't smoked in a year, If ever there was a time I needed one now and went to the cigarette machine and bought a pack. As I opened it, I remembered why I quit, or was forced to when Josh caught me smoking. Lighting up the cigarette, I recalled the night like it was yesterday, Josh and I were camping and I had told him I was going to the bathroom. I was gone for about five minutes when he came looking for me and saw me smoking; the look he gave me was one I never wanted to see again. "What the hell are you doing?" he said as he ripped the cigarette out of my mouth and stepped on it. "Don't you know that shit will kill you? It's not worth it, quit before it's too late." He yelled. I'd never seen him so pissed off. "It's just a cigarette, what's the big deal? It relaxes me and besides it doesn't kill everyone." I snapped back at him. "You willing to take a chance like that, My grandfather died because of smoking. I couldn't stand to watch him suffer the way he did, I don't want to watch you die the same way!" Josh yelled as he hit me knocking me to the ground. "If I ever catch you smoking again, I'll beat the tar out of you, got it!" He said angrily. Picking myself up off the ground I got the distinct feeling he was serious. Josh and I had never fought over anything before and I hurt him that night by doing something stupid. I guess I had forgotten that night until now. "I'm sorry Josh, but I hope you understand how much I need this right now." I said as I inhaled. The cigarette tasted so good; after all I hadn't had one in a year. I sat in the car and just tried to think of how I was going to tell his parents and face his brother. Life's too short and this time it hit too close to home, to me in fact and it hurt a great deal. As I looked around in the car, I felt everything about him, as If he were still here. I started the car and headed home, to an empty road.

We had been about three or four hours away from home, so I didn't have far to travel, but for some reason I wish I were farther away. The closer I got the more scarred I became, I didn't know how to tell them Josh committed suicide. How do you tell someone their son is dead and you could do nothing to stop it? I cried most of the way home; maybe because I was selfish I felt he abandoned me. Josh always had the answer, he knew how to tell someone what needed to be said, and I never could unless I wrote it. That's a big difference between him and I, he had the gift of the spoken word and I the written word. Driving down the open road, I saw kids playing together, friends I gathered, the laughter and happiness they had I missed so much at that moment. The open road was our path to a new life, cut short by tragedy; we planned so much the two of us. I wanted us to be college roommates, all through college. It seemed like nothing would interfere maybe deep inside I hated him for taking those dreams away. How could I be so resentful for something I had no control over? It felt as though I never knew Josh on the inside and I should have. I sat there hating him instead of mourning for him; I was no friend at all.

I got back into town at about four in the afternoon; I pulled over for one last cry before I faced his family. I had hoped that the officer had called ahead and told them, at least to spare me the need to tell them myself. How does one go about telling someone that their son is dead? As I sat on the side of the road, I saw kids playing, the way we did when we were younger. They ran and played without thought of the future. All that mattered to them, was having fun with their friends, something we all take for granted over time. To them, life was complete at that moment in their lives, no worries, not a thing to fear, not even losing those friends around them. Time meant nothing; it was as though it was forever for them. A single tear rolled down my face as I prayed to God for one more day with Josh, knowing I could never have it again. I never really knew, or would know what his last thoughts were, I only could hope he found his peace.

I pulled away looking back at them playing like I looked back on our time we had together, I hoped I never forget the times we shared, the memories within me. I realized why Josh wanted me to write our journey down, he planned this and I see it now. Driving, I feared facing his family, I didn't know what to say, how to act or how to tell them why if asked. I pulled into their driveway and saw them outside, Josh's father holding his wife, I knew that they were informed, and was relieved that I didn't have to be the one to tell them. As I shut the car off, his dad came over to the car sobbing, and trying to hold back his tears. I looked him in the eyes and felt cold within; I still had to face them and everyone who knew him. Opening the door and stepping out, I said, "I'm really sorry. I couldn't stop him, I tried to talk to him but he wouldn't let me help him." His dad put his hand on my shoulder and I knew he didn't blame me for his son's death. "It's not your fault, We should have listened to what he wanted and we know that now. Unfortunately, it's too late. Thanks for being with him, at least someone was with him and that's all that matters right now." His dad said to me wiping his eyes. I saw his mom crying and still shocked at the death of her son, somehow I felt she didn't forgive me. I walked over to her and hugged her as though she were my mother. His mother took it harder, after all, she carried him for nine months and that kind of bond is stronger than any friendship could ever be. The emotional state she was in made me think twice about telling her all Josh had revealed to me. Those words were never told to either of them by me over the years that passed, it was our bond that prevented me from hurting them any further.

I looked for his younger brother, who was no where in sight. Josh and his brother were close, although Josh never admitted it, it showed. "Where's Alex?" I said as I pulled away from her. "He's inside, he's having trouble dealing with all of this, like the rest of us. How are you holding up?" His mom answered. I wasn't exactly sure how to answer her, on the inside I wanted to scream because I wondered how parents could try to run their kids future. Josh never told me how strict they were, if he did I never listened when I should've. I really didn't know how to answer, I was so angry I even blamed him for leaving me alone. "I think I'll go see him, if it's okay?" I asked his Mom. "Don't expect to much, he's not really talking to us either." Josh's mom said to me as I started to the door. I opened the door and walked down the hall past Josh's room; inside was Alex, sitting on his bed looking at a picture of him and Josh at the lake. "I remember when that was taken, you wanted to go with us so bad that day. Josh loved you, I'm sorry about what happened." I said to him as I watched him cry. "Why did you let him die? You should've stopped him." Alex screamed at me. "There was nothing I could do, If there was I would've. I had no idea he would kill himself, please believe me." I said to him as I kneeled in front of him. "You were my brothers best friend and you let him die! How could you just let him die? He always liked you and you did nothing to help him when he needed you." Alex yelled.

Alex was right in a way, I did let Josh down maybe not the way Alex said, but in another way, I should have paid closer attention than I did. I should have seen something was wrong with Josh from the beginning. I watched as Alex cried and I too wanted to cry again, but instead I put my hand on his shoulder and he pulled away. I felt bad enough too, I couldn't believe Alex blamed me, maybe it was my fault. "Get out! Leave me alone and get out, it's your fault my brother's dead, I hate you!" Alex screamed as he threw a picture frame at me. The picture fell to the floor and shattered, the glass went everywhere and even cut my arm. At the time I didn't even notice the cut. I ran as fast as I could out of the house and his parents saw me, and tried to stop me, but I ran all the way home.

When I got home I ran to my room and slammed the door, I didn't even stop to see my mom, she knew I was angry and left me alone. Everything was falling apart around me, if there was ever a time I needed Josh, it was now and I was all alone. I found myself hating him for leaving me and inside I knew it was wrong. I never hated anyone before, nor have I ever lost anyone before either. I sat on my bed staring at the ceiling, thinking about everything we wanted to do together, but never would be able to now. All our plans seemed to fade away, like it was all a dream. The memories of everything we did do together also seemed to be harder to recall it felt as though I was losing everything that ever meant anything to me. I failed him, I failed him was all I kept thinking about. How could I have been so blind to not see the warning signs that he needed me? I sat up and pulled out the necklace and looked at it, he could have had the world I just know it. The eagle flying was indeed like him now. I walked over to the mirror and put it on, I swear to you Josh; I'll never take it off. It was probably the last thing left of Josh that he had before he died, and I owned it now. In a way it felt like Josh was still around with me that night and perhaps he was like he said he would be.

I awoke early the next day, I knew it was the day of the wake, but something inside me still made me feel guilty about what Josh had done. I lay there in bed, still afraid of facing everyone that knew him. It was like the whole world came crashing down on me all at once. I was afraid of what people would say, some may blame me for not being there and I did feel guilty. How could I face all those people, let alone grieve in my own way for the loss of a great friend? Outside, I could hear the birds chirping and the sounds of the neighborhood kids as they played, it was just another day to them, but for me it was like walking to the gallows. I slowly put my feet on the floor and just sat there thinking about Josh and how much I already missed him. Josh always was the first one to get up when he slept over; I remember when he tried to wake me up one morning using a squirt gun. He soaked me good, which made me wide-awake that morning. Josh enjoyed playing games like that; it was just the way he was. We used to try to out do the other each morning with something different. Unfortunately, it was usually me that caught got the wake up call. I never could get up before him, except now.

I was startled by the knocking on my bedroom door, "Come in." I said half-awake. The door opened slowly, and Jeremy poked his head inside. "I came as soon as I heard, are you okay?" Jeremy replied. "I'm okay. Thanks for asking." I said to him. "I can't believe what happened. Did he say anything to you?" Jeremy asked. "We talked for awhile, and after that he went for a walk. I dozed off for a little while until he came back, he told me not to worry and go to sleep, he said he'd see me in the morning and that was the last time I saw him alive." I told him. "I guess you found him the next morning. It's not your fault, there wasn't anything you could've done so don't blame yourself." Jeremy said to me. "Yeah, I found him, I just stood there unable to speak or move. I still see him in the tub, I can't get it out of my head." I answered. "You may never get it out of your head, but you can keep telling yourself that it's not your fault. Maybe it will make it easier to deal with." Jeremy said out of concern. "Everytime I close my eyes, I see him there in front of me dead, it hurts a great deal. I failed him, I should have stayed awake that night, none of this would have happened." I said crying. "You can't blame yourself, Josh wouldn't want that. I know you two were close friends, and you can't blame yourself for something that you couldn't control. He was lucky enough to have you with him instead of dying alone. Don't take that away from him." Jeremy replied. Jeremy sat down across from me, I knew he meant well and I couldn't stop crying. "So many questions run through my mind, I just can't stop thinking about him. I wish I had another chance." I sobbed. "You did. You had what his parents didn't, the last minutes of his life. He was lucky to have you as a friend so don't take that away from him." Replied Jeremy. I listened to what he was saying, and I knew he was right but I still felt as though I failed him. Jeremy was similar to Josh, I felt comfortable being able to talk to someone. I only wished Josh trusted me more than he did, maybe he'd be alive today.

My life changed forever, I would never have a friend like the one I had with Josh. That day changed everything, I changed inside. They say in a lifetime you're lucky to have one great friend, true friends are hard to come by. Josh was that friend; no one could replace him ever. "I'd better get going, I just wanted to see if you're okay. I'll see you at the wake tonight, if you need a ride call." Jeremy said as he left. I got dressed and sat there for a time, trying to understand all that happened. I heard the phone ring and picked it up on the second ring.

"Hello?" I said. The voice at the other end was Josh's father, "How you doing Jim? I was wondering if you would like to say a few words tonight at the wake?" he said. "You mean a speech, I wouldn't know what to say. I guess I could come up with something." I answered. "Great. Josh would like that; after all you two were close friends. I'll see you tonight." He said as he hung up. I tried to remember what he meant to me and how he treated others, maybe that would be a great beginning. I got dressed and decided to go for a ride to think, I needed time to be alone for a while so I could stay in control at the wake. Driving was really a great way to think and relax it was something we did often together. As I passed the funeral parlor, I realized it wasn't a dream, it was really happening. I felt somehow as though I failed Josh as a friend, like I did nothing to help him.

CHAPTER 4

The parking lot to the funeral parlor was full, teachers, students, friends, and relatives all gathered to pay their last respects to a fallen friend. I sat in the car just watching all the people and listening to a song that Josh always played whenever we went anywhere, he said it reminded him of who we really are on the inside. I felt nervous about facing everyone, I figured they may blame me and in a sense they were right. As I walked slowly from the parking lot I could hear all the voices around me talking at once. Everyone seemed to stare at me, or through me as though I was to blame, I felt cold, like I didn't belong here tonight. I knew people would blame me for his death, I mean I was the last one with him and I should've realized what was happening, but I didn't. In a sense, I did fail my friend. Josh had never let me down in all the time we knew each other and for the first time I let him and his family down. Guilt has a way of creeping up on someone, it's like someone's twisting a knife inside you and the pain just keeps getting deeper and deeper.

I entered the funeral parlor and signed the guest book, then proceeded to make my way through the crowd to Josh's casket. As I approached, I couldn't hold back anymore the tears formed inside and slowly rolled down the side of my face. I reached for Josh's hand and held it not wanting to ever let go of the only friend I ever had in my entire life. Everything hit me at that moment, it grew inside me and I could no longer hold back what was lost. I missed him so much, all his wisdom, his jokes, his sense of humor, even how he always managed to make me laugh when I had a bad day. Josh was what held me together all these years; he gave me a sense of hope when it felt as though there was none to be found. All the thought's of us being together suddenly rushed into me and I relived those moments as though they were happening all over again. "Josh, I'm going to miss you friend, you gave me more than you'll ever realize. I'll never find anyone like you in my lifetime." I said to him as I loosened my grip from his hand. I stood there for a moment holding the necklace he had left me as though it were in fact a part of him that I know possessed. For a moment, in my mind I could actually see Josh flying among the clouds finally free.

The people passed through the family line all giving their condolences for the loss of Josh. Many people cried, while some tried like I did to hold it together for the sake of the family. I walked over to take my place in the line as I was asked to by Josh's dad. I didn't feel right about being in the family line but Josh's dad said we were close friends and that made me a part of the family even though Josh's brother still blamed me. Josh's brother gave me a cold stare and then walked off, I could see the hate in his eyes and all I could do was put my head down in shame. "Alex, come back here right now." Josh's dad said as he walked off. "I'm sorry Jim, he still can't deal with his brother's death. I'm sure he don't really blame you, It's just going to take some time." His dad said. "I know, I'll go talk to him. I want to explain what happened, I owe him that." I said. "Just don't expect him to listen, it will take a while" his dad said. I saw him walk towards the hall and followed him until I caught up with him.

I saw him sitting in the corner crying all curled up as though he could hide from everyone else. "Alex, can we please talk?" I said to him putting my hand on his shoulder. "It's all your fault! Why didn't you do anything? Why weren't you there when he needed you, why?" Alex cried. "I tried to listen, I didn't know he'd commit suicide. You've got to believe me. I never would have let your brother hurt himself had I known. He was my best friend and I didn't know." I said to him as I sat beside him. "You shouldn't have left him alone. When he needed you, you weren't there. He trusted you." Alex sobbed wiping his eyes. I sat there thinking about that night, Josh wasn't right and I saw that to late. I only thought about our trip and couldn't see passed anything else. Maybe Alex was right; maybe I was only thinking of myself and not seeing the truth right in front of me. "Why don't we go outside for a while so you can dry your eyes and we can talk." I said standing up and reaching out my hand to Alex. Alex took my hand and stood up, wiping his eyes and following me to the door.

Once outside, we went over to the side of the building for a little privacy. "I never meant for anything to happen to Josh, I hurt too. I know what you feel even if you don't believe me." I said lighting up a cigarette. I remembered how Josh yelled at me for smoking. "What are you thinking about?" Alex asked as I stood in silence. "Well, your brother yelled at me for smoking, and here I am smoking at his funeral. I can just imagine what he's saying right now." I said sitting down. “I’m sure he only cared about your health, I don’t think he was mad at you.” Alex said. “That was what made your brother so great, he always thought of others before himself. Your brother meant everything to me, as he did to you. Do you really blame me or are you just angry inside?” I asked. “It hurts. I don’t blame you directly, I’m sorry for that.” Alex said to me. We both sat there for a while just thinking, I had never really talked to Josh’s brother the way I did and I realized a little of Josh was right beside me. Josh was a great friend, and I wish I had that second chance to change that night. Inside we both still hurt a great deal we both had to deal with the loss in our own way. Alex stood up and said, “I’m really sorry I blamed you, I didn’t mean it. I hope you’ll still come by and visit us.” I stood up and was relieved that things were better between Alex and I. “Someone’s got to look after you, I think Josh would be pissed if I never came around to see you any more.” I said to him. It’s funny, even though Alex wasn’t mad at me, I was still angry myself that Josh left me behind all alone. Everything I thought I could accomplish seemed to mean nothing without him there to support me, maybe that sounds selfish but it was the truth and a part of me hated him for leaving me. I wasn’t quite sure how to get on with my life, especially since we both were always together to support each other’s dreams. We planned so much that we never realized those dreams may never come true.

Alex had gone back inside before me and I stood outside alone, crying to myself. It hit me all the sudden that all our dreams were shattered and I may have been able to change the outcome of that night after all. All those times that Josh had been there for me and when he needed me the most I wasn’t there for him. The rage built up inside me like it was alive, as though it was real and I needed to get it out. I screamed outloud and fell to my knees crying like I had never done before. Andy was close by and came running over to me and I just stood up and without thinking shoved him into the wall. “What’s wrong, are you all right?” He asked standing up. “It’s all my fault! I should’ve done something to stop him; I should’ve seen it coming. I did nothing to help and now look what’s happened.” I screamed. Without thinking, I ran into the street and was struck by a car. As I lay there in the street, all I thought about was Josh before I lost consciousness.

Even though I was unable to open my eyes, I could hear everything around me. I heard the crowd ask if I was dead, I knew I wasn't and a part of me wished I was, so I could tell Josh how sorry I was for what had happened. I hurt inside as well as outside, The driver yelled that he didn't even see me. Andy was at my side and I felt him lift my hand and tell me to hold on, that help was on the way. I wanted to die for what I had done to Josh, I felt so responsible for his death. I prayed for my own death right where I lay, all the while Andy yelled it's not your time hold on please hold on. The ambulance arrived and I could hear them ask what happened, the driver asked if Andy was the witness and said that he'd have to fill out an accident report with the police. By this time, a large crowd had gathered outside, it wasn't enough that my friend lay inside a casket, but that I had tried to take my own life right outside. Inside, I knew what I was doing as I ran into the street. I wanted forgiveness for my loss and knew I would never again see him, I risked my own life to gain his forgiveness.

Andy held on to my hand all the way to the hospital, I felt like he was keeping me from being free as Josh was. I wanted to die so bad that I guess it wasn't my time and I didn't understand why. "Why won't he wake up? What's wrong with him?" Andy asked the medic. "He's got some trauma to his head and back injuries. I'm not sure if he'll walk again, his spine may be broke." The medic said. "Is he going to live?" Andy asked. "If we got to him in time and I think we did. Just don't move him at all." The medic replied putting an intravenous tube in my arm. I was aware of everything around me, but I couldn't speak or open my eyes. In a way, it was like being dead, not in the sense of death itself, but aware and unable to tell anyone I was still inside. I needed to come to terms with the events past and maybe this was my punishment for my mistake I made. The ambulance arrived at the hospital and they all rushed me inside, Andy still holding my hand never once letting go, like Josh would have done for me. On the inside I still hurt badly, I still blamed myself and wouldn't let it go. I caused his death, and now I will pay for what I did to him and his family, justice served.

I over heard the staff say my back was broken in two places and there was swelling on my vertebrae. The doctors told Andy that through physical therapy I might have a chance to walk again. To me, I wished I'd have died, it didn't matter if I walked again and maybe that would be punishment enough to pay back Josh for me not being there for him. I decided then that God would punish me for my actions as he saw fit. Jeremy arrived later that night, I heard his voice as Andy told him what happened. "Why don't you go home and get some rest, I'll stay with him through the night and we'll switch in the morning." Jeremy said to Andy. "Are you sure, I can stay longer. I don't want to leave him now." Andy said. "You can't do any more than I can, go home and sleep, I'll call if there's any change I swear. Besides, The doctors said he could be in a coma for some time." Jeremy replied. Andy gave Jeremy my hand and Jeremy looked at him in confusion, "He knows were here, just hold his hand so he knows were here for him." Andy replied. "Okay, I'll do that. Will you please just go home and get some sleep?" Jeremy asked Andy. I heard Andy say good bye as he left and I saw him in my mind the way I did at my birthday party. My mind filled with everything that had happened over the past several weeks, even before Josh's death. It was as though I was reliving everything, a chance to see my friends and especially Josh the way I should've always seen them.

Jeremy never left my side that night; he still had my hand, as though it were a life line keeping me on the right path in the road ahead. "Why did you pull such a dumb stunt? Why didn't you talk to us?" Jeremy said in my ear. I wanted to answer, I wanted to tell him that I did blame myself for not doing something more for Josh that night, but I couldn't answer him. The room was quiet, except for the machines that I was hooked up to, which meant that Jeremy fell asleep at my side never letting go of my hand the entire time. My friends gave up a lot for me that night. I felt I should've done the same for Josh, maybe things would've been different.

The next morning, Jeremy awoke and still had my hand. "I'm still here waiting for you to comeback where you belong. Please wake up,We all need you." Jeremy whispered in my ear. The doctors kept coming in and checking the machines all day long, with no obvious changes. Jeremy had left and I was alone. My parents had come in for a while, but they were told there's nothing they could really do either until I came out of the coma on my own. I felt so secure that I didn't want to wake up, I had the time to think and wonder about whether or not I could have changed anything. I was the only one that was there the night Josh committed suicide, and I had to know if I could've changed anything that night. I had to live with what happened because no one else was there except for me. That in itself was a heavy price to be weighed on one's conscience.

CHAPTER 5

The day's seemed to pass quickly, maybe because they were all the same to me at the time. People came in, and people left. I knew they were there, but yet I still thought about that night. Again I wanted to scream, but I couldn't. I finally wanted out of my shell, I knew it would soon be time to face the world around me and get help in dealing with Josh's death, I was afraid. If ever I needed Josh, it was right now. Somehow, having Josh around things always seemed to work out in the end. Josh had a way of making people believe in themselves even when all seemed lost. Josh and I had been through a lot together, he even helped me one night when I attended a party and had too much to drink. Josh drove me back to his house and let me stay there, he even called my parents and came up with a great excuse as to why I wasn't coming home that night. If it weren't for Josh, I could have been killed myself had I drove home that night.

I awoke to find Jeremy still holding onto my hand, fast asleep in the chair beside me. I couldn't move much at all, except my hand so I squeezed his hard to let him know I was back. Jeremy stirred almost instantly and jumped back, forgetting he still had my hand. I winced in pain as he then realized and let go. "Your awake!" He screamed. I could only mumble because my voice was hoarse from the tubes that had been in my throat. "How long have I been out for?" I asked. "Two weeks, It's been two weeks. How do you feel?" Jeremy asked me. "I don't. I can't move, what's wrong with me." I asked. "You broke your back and you have some swelling on your spine. The doctors said it's up to you if you'll ever walk again. The break has healed slightly, but the swelling isn't completely gone." Jeremy explained. I lay there not really listening, but instead thinking about the fact that I missed the funeral of my best friend. "Are you listening to what I said, it's important that you try or you may never walk again." Jeremy replied. "How was the funeral?" I stated finally. "I'd worry more about you right now. You're in no condition to worry about that yet." Jeremy firmly stated. "I asked you a question, now answer me! My best friend is dead, and you think I care about what happened to me, answer the dam question." I said harshly. "The funeral was nice, everything went well. I took your place as a bearer and helped carry Josh." Jeremy answered. I was still angry inside and

I took out my anger on him, even though I knew it was not his fault. "I thought we were friends, I've been here almost everyday waiting for you. How many times do you have to be told it wasn't you're fault that Josh died." Jeremy yelled. "I was the last one with him that night, everyone else must blame me. Why not just accept the blame and take the punishment that goes along with it, maybe everyone will be glad I paid for not being there when I should've done something." I replied.

I lay there with my head and body basically immobile, a single tear rolling down my face. "So that's it then? You're just going to give up on yourself, and everything else. What about your book, you just going to throw it away too." Jeremy asked me. "How am I supposed to live with myself? My friend died and I did nothing to help him. How can I go on with my life always thinking that maybe I could have done something." I replied to Jeremy. Jeremy just sat there shaking his head, I knew he meant well, but I still felt the same way as I did. I didn't see things the way I was supposed to, I missed the clues and I was no friend to him that night. I felt I deserved the punishment I received and I was satisfied with the judgement given to me. Jeremy stood up and came over to the bed and slammed his fists down on the table violently. "You may want to give upon yourself, but I swear I'll force you to fight and want to live!" Jeremy yelled. "Oh, and how do you intend to do that? You can't force me to change my mind about anything. Give it your best shot." I answered him. "I'll find a way, giving up on yourself isn't going to bring Josh back! You have to go on with your life, he'd want you to and you know that. Fight for you and him, don't give up!" Jeremy yelled. I lay there shocked at the words that Jeremy had said, I'd never seen him like that before and I knew he wasn't going to let up at all. I did want to skate with Jeremy again, but I was too afraid that Josh would hate me for living without him.

Jeremy refused to leave right away, even though I had treated him like shit. He sure was stubborn which made him a lot like me actually. I too was set in my ways so we were both at a stalemate. We waited for the other to make the next move, the move that would or wouldn't change the future. "Why don't you rest for awhile, Jim. I'll be here when you wake up and we'll talk more later." Jeremy said as he removed his shoes and put his feet on the bed. Out of the corner of my eye Jeremy fell asleep and I too tried to sleep. I was afraid in a way to close my eyes; I kept reliving the day I had found Josh. I didn't know what to do, for a time I just sat there in shock, hoping it was just a practical joke, but it wasn't. I had always tried to be there for him, unfortunately, this time I failed and it cost Josh his life.

I finally managed to doze off for a few hours and when I awoke, Jeremy was still there fast asleep as he said he would be. Jeremy never broke his word; he always stuck to his promise, even if he got in trouble for doing it. Not being able to move was something I wasn't used to, I wanted to get up, but my body wouldn't cooperate. The only part of my body I could move was my hands and my head, barely enough to look around the room. I wished I had Josh right now, maybe he could've helped make things easier to deal with. I managed to move my hand across Jeremy's foot to wake him. "Did you sleep Jim?" Jeremy asked. "Yeah I did. Thanks for staying with me." I answered. "Are you ready to talk or are you still going to be stubborn?" Jeremy replied. "I want to try, but I'm afraid. I still hurt on the inside and I still blame myself. The nightmares won't go away." I said. "The doctors suggest you see a Psychologist before you begin further treatment, maybe it'll help you deal with the loss of Josh." Jeremy stated. "I don't need a shrink, I can handle it." I replied turning my head away. "Oh you can huh, look what you did, are you forgetting you tried to kill yourself. You ran right in front of a car and you call this being able to deal with it." Jeremy said raising his voice. "I freaked out, I didn't try to kill my self. I just started running, I wasn't paying attention where I was going until it was too late." I stated. "Well, it sure looked like you tried to kill yourself to the rest of us. Josh wouldn't want you to blame yourself, so why do you?" Jeremy asked. "You weren't there that night, I was." I said.

I knew Jeremy meant well, but no one else but me saw the look in his eyes. Even though I saw it, I didn't think he'd do anything about it, I should've realized that he hurt more than he let on and I ignored his plea for help. For all I know, Josh may have hated me for not seeing through him and doing more than I did for him that night. I can't to this day forget that I may have let my friend down that night, I was with him and all I could think about was the trip, my friend needed me and I wasn't there to help him. In my mind, I failed him I was to blame for his death and I was determined not to let anyone tell me any different. Because Josh and I were close friends, he tried to let me in, he wanted my help but I didn't see it. Many people are never let in they are turned away when they offer help, but Josh was different he turned to me and I in turn ignored him. I was given the chance to help him with his problems and my selfishness caused him to make an irrational decision that cost him his life. The things that went on in my mind cannot be understood by anyone but me, now I too feel as Josh did that night, all alone. Friends like Josh are in deed hard to come by, they come once in a lifetime and I lost out on the best friend that life gave me.

The sun had gone down, and the moon light shined through the window lighting up the room. "It's getting late, maybe I should go home tonight. You seem to be better and you could use the rest." Jeremy said. A part of me wanted him to leave, but another part of me didn't. "No, I'd like you to stay. I didn't mean to yell, I wish you could understand how I feel. I found him and all these thoughts went through my mind." I said. "You're right, I don't know what it's like to find a friend like that, but talking about can help. If you want me to stay, I'll stay but you have to agree to talk to a professional. If you do it, it will help you to clear your head for the long road ahead of you." Jeremy said as he shook my hand. "Agreed. How long will I have to see a shrink for before I can begin the physical therapy?" I asked him. "Now that the swelling has gone down, it won't be long. The doctors are going to try putting you in a wheel chair in the morning, at least it's a start." Jeremy told me. "Are you going to be here for that or are you going to leave? I could use the support." I replied. "I'll be here, I start classes tomorrow and I'll only be able to come by every couple of days." Jeremy said. I had forgotten that Jeremy signed up for summer college courses. With those final thought's, I fell asleep and Jeremy fell asleep in the chair as well.

I awoke early the next day, just as the doctors came in the room. "So, how are you feeling today?" The doctor said. "As well as can be, considering the circumstances." I said. The doctor pulled up the other chair and sat down opposite Jeremy, trying not to wake him. "Looks like your friend's really tired, you guys didn't stay awake too late did you?" He said. "No, We talked for awhile. Jeremy's been here for a few days straight, he hasn't been home." I said to the doctor. "You've got some friend there, to stay as long as he did." The doctor replied. "Yeah, I guess I do don't I. So, I hear I'll be seeing a shrink soon. I also hear I'll be put in a wheel chair as well." I asked him. "Yes, to both questions. But first, I want to X-ray your back to be sure the swelling is down enough before we move you. It won't take long." The doctor said as he moved in the machine.

The X-ray machine was a portable unit, which made it sometimes easier for the medical staff to bring the machine to patients that could not move. As the technician moved in the machine, the doctor removed the hospital gown, which was totally embarrassing and not to mention humiliating. The doctor realized how uncomfortable it was for me and pulled the covers up to my waste covering up what I didn't really want to be seen by to many people. "Okay, we are going to take a few pictures of your back and find out exactly how well your healing. Just relax and take a deep breath when you're told to, and hold it until we tell you different." The doctor said. At about this time, Jeremy started to wake up finally realizing what was going on, he quickly moved into the hall so they could finish their work. "How long before I know the results?" I asked. "Within the hour, if all goes well and I don't foresee a problem." The doctor answered as he told the technician to rush the results. "What happens if everything's okay? I asked him. "Well, first you'll see the shrink, then you'll begin physical therapy so we can get you back on your feet. I'll be back in an hour or so with the results for you." The doctor said leaving. I overheard Jeremy stop the doctor, after all the hall had an echo and it wasn't hard to hear what was said. "Doctor, I'm concerned, do you think he will be able to walk. He's been really depressed about Josh's death and I think he'll not even try." Jeremy asked. "I'm sure he'll walk again, but only if he tries. I can't force someone that doesn't want to. We have to give it time." The doctor said to him. As Jeremy entered the room, I played dumb even though I heard all that was said and still had my doubts.

The last thing I had remembered before the accident was walking up to the casket and seeing Josh laying there motionless and expression less, in a way I saw myself. It was like looking at a mirror and seeing the future and that can cause a person to snap on the inside. Seeing someone like that can cause a persons mind to reexamine one's life, often times the way a person lived his life and if it was worth it to him. I was supposed to be a pallbearer as well as Josh's brother, father and uncle. The family said that Josh would've wanted that, and I really wanted to give him that respect and final wish. My emotions took over causing me to make a harsh judgement and resulting in my current situation. I failed Josh not once, but twice as well as his family. The funeral had been over for a few weeks and I still didn't get to say good bye to the greatest friend I had ever known in my entire life. No one told me about the funeral, or the service and I lost the opportunity to pay my final respects in private. I wanted to see him one more time before it was too late, and now it is too late. I wished I could go back and have that one moment with Josh that I long desired before he was laid to rest in peace. I wanted to make my peace with him, even to ask for his forgiveness for what happened that night. As a Pallbearer, friend or family the closing of the casket is a time to make that eternal peace with the loved one, it's actually the everlasting picture of that person you hold deep in your heart forever.

Jeremy came back into the room and sat down beside the bed, he seemed to make it his bed for the past several days. "Keep your fingers crossed that the news is in your favor." He said. "How was the funeral?" I asked abruptly. "What do you mean, it was a funeral." Jeremy replied as if trying to avoid the subject. "I mean was it a good one, was the service nice, who took my place. I need to know, I never got to say good bye the way everyone else did, and I feel empty inside." I answered. No one bothered to ever tell me about the funeral, maybe they were trying to avoid upsetting me or maybe they just felt I had enough to deal with, either way I needed to know and now was the time to find out how things went that afternoon. The emptiness I felt inside had been eating at me for days, and I just needed to know that Josh was finally at peace and that he had a nice service, even if I couldn't have been there. "Everyone showed up to the wake, family and his friends from school. The funeral was very good, the service was a great tribute to him and the graveside service was equally nice." Jeremy replied with hesitation in his voice. For some reason, he still didn't answer my other question; it was as if he was hiding something from me. "Who took my place as pallbearer? I really would like to know." I asked him straight out. "I did. I'm sorry for that but it was a last minute decision because of what happened to you." Jeremy finally answered me. "At least one of us was there for him. I'm not mad, I just wish I could have done it. I wanted to say good bye to him, but not this way." I said to him.

I needed to say good bye to my friend, but with the situation that I was in, that was not possible. Inside, I began to understand what had to be done in order for me to make my final peace with Josh; the only thing stopping me from doing that was awaiting the results of the X-ray. I didn't realize how losing a friend could eat you alive on the inside. I thought I could deal with everything but somehow my on guilt was my worst enemy. I began to pray that the results would come back in my favor so that I could have the courage to face the fact that my friend was gone forever. I wanted to go to his grave and just sit there and tell him how sorry I was for that night, right now it was only a dream. Jeremy assured me, that eventually I would be able to get on with my life, it just takes time to heal the wounds inside as well as the outside. "Maybe if all goes well, you will be able to walk to Josh's grave and make up for what you feel you missed." Jeremy said as I was looking out the window. "I wish things were different, I should've thought about what I did before I did it." I answered. "Yeah, you should've, but that's in the past. You have to have faith that things will work out in the end. Josh would want you to go on, as well as finish your book." Jeremy said pulling it out of the drawer. I turned my head to see him placing it on the bed beside me. "Right now, I can only think about how much I miss him. We had a lot of fun over the 'm afraid I'll lose those memories." I said. "No one said it would be easy. I miss him too, as well as his family. We have to go on there's no other way about it, but that doesn't mean you have to forget all the two of you did together." Jeremy said. A single tear again rolled down my face.

Some one once said that time heals all wounds, no matter how deep. I can only pray that saying is true because all I had was time ahead of me. Lying in bed was starting to really get to me; I wanted to get away from my room that felt more like a prison than anything else to me at the time. It was as though I was being held against my will and everyone else controlled my every move. The world around me went on as though nothing happened, but it felt like I was the only one to see things for what they were. Jeremy had been a real friend to me, but somehow it wasn't the same. I didn't want to be rude or even hurt his feelings but I needed Josh, that would never change. Often enough, I cried myself to sleep some nights more than others. I often felt like I was truly alone now, Josh was the only one that knew what to do, I never had to make my own choices. Now I had to start making them and hope they were the right ones.

It had been over an hour, past the time the doctor had said and I began to feel hopeless inside. The longer I had to wait seemed as though the results weren't in fact in my favor. "I'm not going to leave you, no matter what the results are we'll work through it I promise." Jeremy said as he took my hand and squeezed tight. It was the kind of handshake a person knew was true to heart and would never be broken. I felt a little better, but not as much as I would've if the doctor would show up sooner. At about that time, Alex knocked at the door. "You're awake. It's good to see you, I'm sorry I didn't come down sooner but things have been a little difficult for us." He said entering the room. "I understand. And I'm glad to see you're still talking to me. How you doing?" I said to Alex. "I'm better. I miss him, as do my Mom and Dad. I also was told by Jeremy in more detail and I really don't blame you, I want to be friends." Alex replied. That was so far the greatest relief I had in a while. To hear those words meant a lot and in a way, I could actually see Josh inside his brother Alex. The two looked a lot alike, I never noticed that before now.

Jeremy had left the room so Alex and I could talk things out. We talked for about a half-hour before the doctor finally came in with the results. "Maybe I should leave, so you can have some privacy." Alex said suddenly. "No, You can stay. I want you to hear this, no matter how they are." I said as the doctor sat down. "I promised I'd wait until you're other friend got back. He wanted to be here to, okay?" The doctor said to me. "I've waited this long, a little longer won't hurt much." I said. Not long after the doctor had said that, Jeremy came rushing in as though he was going to miss out on what the doctor was going to say. "Did I miss anything?" Jeremy said out of breath. "No, the doctor said we were to wait for you. I hope it's not bad news, doc?" I said. "Okay, now that we are all here let's get started. First, the swelling has gone down enough for your treatment to start." The doctor said. "That's great." Jeremy and Alex said in unison. I breathed a sigh of relief and whispered to myself, thanks Josh. For some reason I felt as though he was with me that night. "I've also decided against you seeing a shrink, as you call it. Instead, I want you to attend group therapy, I think that will better suit your needs. The group meets before and after therapy sessions to discuss each others progress and to help comfort each other." The doctor said. "When can Jim get started with therapy?" Jeremy asked. "Well, how about in two days. I think that will give you enough time to prepare yourself and meet a person that's been through something similar as you." The doctor said as he stood up. "Congratulations Jim." Alex said shaking my hand. "Thanks. Maybe I will be able to finally pay my respects to your brother." I answered. "Well, I'll leave you three alone. If you have any questions please call the nurse's station and I'll get in touch with you. I think you two can go home tonight and get some sleep, Jim will be fine and he's going to need time alone to think." The doctor said to them. "Maybe he's right, we'll be back tomorrow night and we can talk some more." Jeremy said. "Actually, I was thinking, seeing as how you're doing so good would you like to go for a short ride in the wheel chair with your friends before we call it a night?" The doctor asked. "What do you say Jim, you feel up to it? We promise to be careful." Jeremy said. "Sounds great, I've been wanting to get out of this room for some time." I said. Finally things were starting to look up for me; I was finally going to be able to apologize to Josh in person.

The doctor left the room to get a wheel chair and came back a short time later. "How about your friends help you into the chair. I've already told the staff you have permission to be out for one hour, be careful and if there are any problems find a nurse and she'll help you. Jeremy, you support his back and lift him into the chair. Remember it's his legs that are not working now. Alex you swing his feet and legs down, carefully so you don't drop them, he can still break them if you're not careful." The doctor instructed. Jeremy sat behind me and lifted my body so it rested against his chest. "You okay so far, Jim." Jeremy said. "Yes, it's okay. I don't feel to much pain." I answered. Jeremy slid me into the chair holding my waist at the same time. The only thing left to do was move my legs and Alex did just that, carefully. Alex lifted one foot at a time into the foot rest. "Are you ready for a trip around the hospital, in style of course?" Jeremy said laughing. "For tonight, we will be your drivers, sir. Where to?" Alex replied. "Well let's just start with this floor, then we'll move on down." I said with a smile. "Were off then. Thanks doctor, we'll take care of him and have him back soon." Jeremy said as he wheeled me out. For the first time in about a week, I felt free, and I couldn't wait to see beyond this room.

Alex followed close behind as we made our way past the nurse's station, everyone there smiled as though I was a miracle. I knew I hadn't been the easiest patient, and everyone still stood by me to support me whether I liked it or not. It was great the way Alex and Jeremy didn't give up on me, I didn't think I was worth the effort. Sometimes, I guess others see things better then we do, giving it all the more reason for them to push us forward so we don't give up. The nurse's gave Jeremy a pillow to put behind my back so I would be more comfortable and each of us a cup of soda. As we proceeded on our maiden voyage, we came upon a window and Jeremy stopped so I could look out into the world and see what I hadn't seen for some time, the world around me. To me, it looked like a trophy that I had to have, or maybe a new achievement that was ahead of me. I realized the dream of walking again was a lot closer than I ever thought would be. "Look at all the people down there, they look like ants from up here." Alex pointed out. It was a full moon out, which made the night look so bright. In the near distance I saw a fork in the road, similar to the one I had described to Josh the night we talked in the hotel. I knew it had become my fork in the road, my chance to decide my fate.

We moved along down the hall past the patient's rooms and to the elevator. As we waited for the elevator, Jeremy and Alex smiled at me and laughed, I wasn't sure as to what they were up to but I knew it was no good. With these two, one could only imagine as to what awaited me. "What's so funny?" I asked. "Nothing, it's just great to see you in a better mood then you were earlier. You're finally making some progress and you should be proud of yourself." Jeremy answered. "Do you realize how close you are to making a complete recovery?" Alex noted as he kneeled down to my level. "Yeah, I do. I just hope that I can make a complete recovery." I answered him. The doors opened and I was wheeled in and Alex pushed the button down one floor. As the doors closed it reminded me of what it must have looked like as they closed the casket on Josh the day of the funeral. I can just imagine the emptiness of being sealed up forever. Jeremy put his hand on my shoulder as though he knew what I was thinking, maybe he understood me or maybe I just wanted him too. The doors opened up to a long hall way, it was like I could see my goals ahead of me but it was like I couldn't reach them no matter how hard I tried. "I think I'm at war with myself." I said suddenly. "What do you mean by that Jim." Alex asked. "Well, A part of me wants to walk again, but another part wants me to accept things the way they are as punishment. Does it make any sense at all or am I crazy." I explained to him. "I think it's just nerves, you're a little afraid of the therapy and scared that it may not work. It will work, it will be hard work and painful and even frustrating, but you can't give up." Jeremy replied.

We made our way down the hall, all of us silent for a short time, reflecting on what was the truth.

I was given a second chance in life, what I choose to do with that was up to me. It was like history repeating itself, but only with me instead of Josh. I told him about the fork in the road and now I was face to face with the same life decision that would change me forever, I had to make the right choice for me and accept the consequences, no matter what they may be. I knew the road ahead wasn't going to be easy, but I had to try for two reasons. The first, for me to walk again, the second, to make up for my mistake to Josh. I wanted to tell him everything and ask for his forgiveness. Jeremy continued to wheel me around with Alex following close behind, this floor didn't have much to look at but we made use of the time away from my room anyway. "I need to find a bathroom, quickly." Jeremy said. We went down the next corridor, and finally found one. Jeremy parked me outside the door and went in leaving me alone with Alex. Alex held out his closed hand and said, "I think it's time you wore this again." He opened his hand and in it was the chain Josh left for me. He put it around my neck, I thought I had lost it. The day I woke up, I couldn't find it, I though someone stole it or I had lost it. "Where did you find it? I thought I lost that." I asked him. "It was in the road after you got hit by the car, and I found it and held on to it for you until it was the right time for you to wear it again. I also read the note that was in your pocket, I'm sorry for that but I know understand how close you and my brother were." Alex said. "Thanks a lot. I really appreciate that." I answered as I held the charm in my hand. Jeremy came out and we continued on our trip to the elevator.

Having the necklace again made the realization of the goals ahead of me more realistic and achievable. I felt stronger inside because I knew then that Josh would be with me forever. I even felt his presence there with us. I never told either of them about that at all, I didn't think they'd believe me. The elevator was up ahead and we pressed on as if it was a doorway to what lay ahead of us. "How you doing so far, Jim." Jeremy asked. "Great, I feel fine and can't wait to start therapy." I replied. "Just remember, don't expect instant success right away, it will take time." Jeremy said to me. "I know, but at least now I have a better chance." I answered. We entered the elevator and headed down another flight to the next floor, hoping it was more interesting than the last one. To our surprise, it was it was the cafeteria and we were all starving. I guess this hospital food will have to do. “So what should we get, my treat.” Alex said. “Where did you get that kind of money?” Jeremy asked. “I saved my allowance for weeks, why not spend it on something worth while.” Alex explained to us. “It’s settled then, let’s eat. Alex and I will get us all diner and bring it back to the table, you wait here okay?” Jeremy asked. I sat in the chair at the table closest to the window, which provided a great view of the street below.

As I sat there, I saw the same fork in the road as I did above us and prayed that the choice I was to make would eventually pay off, all the while never letting go of the charm on the chain. The cafeteria wasn’t to busy, so it didn’t take long for them to return with dinner, consisting of a teen’s favorite diet, burgers, fries and soda. God it felt great to eat real food again. We sat there and ate our dinner, and I looked around at the people next to us and saw them crying. It seems they were crying for joy, Their son came out of surgery and was going to live. I was very happy for them and knew they were too, it showed in there expression. “Thanks again, for dinner. This sure beats what they’ve been feeding me upstairs.” I told him. I had been cooped up in my room for so long, that I had forgotten what good food was like as well as having friends around me again. “I’ll have to leave later on, I start school tomorrow, but I’ll try to come by as often as I can. If you need anything before then, call and I’ll see what I can do.” Jeremy said. “Thanks for everything. I appreciate it a lot; I should be all right. I hope you do well in classes this semester.” I answered. “You nervous about starting your therapy?” Alex asked. “A little, but If I don’t try, I already let your brother down and I’ve done that too much already. I want to see your brother’s grave, and I want to be able to walk there on my own.” I replied. “He’d be glad that you’re finally using your head. I’m sure you’ll do fine, but don’t give up, the first few sessions won’t be easy.” Alex said. We finished eating; it was getting pretty late so we decided to head back to my room.

As we were heading upstairs, I started to remember how Josh and I used to spend a lot of time together, the nights we had were really important to both of us. We used to sit up for hours and just talk, something everyone does except for us it was different, we both listened to each other and gave each other advice on how to deal with our situations. Josh and I often went to the quarries and just sat on the beach, having a beer together and just listening to the radio. I guess I was luckier than I realized those memories and all the others I still had them alive inside me. I wished that I understood at the time how important those nights were to both of us. The elevator doors opened on my floor, and it was only a short time before we reached my room. Jeremy and Alex helped me back into my bed and then they sat for awhile with me. I really didn't want them to leave but it was getting late and after all they had done so much for me. "Well, we should be going. I'll give Alex a ride home. You, need to get some sleep tomorrow's your big day. I'll call you tomorrow night to see how you made out." Jeremy said as he shook my hand. "Yeah, I hope you do well. I'll see you soon." Alex said standing up. "Thanks again guys it felt good to get out for a while." I said as they headed towards the door. Before long, they were gone and I was alone. After they left, I noticed that Jeremy had left the book I had been writing on the table beside me, I reached over and leafed through what I had written. I couldn't believe how close I was to actually finishing the book. I knew that eventually I would have to finish it so I wouldn't break a promise I had made to Josh right before he died. He said that I owed it to myself to finish what I had started. It would be the only way I would now if I had what it takes to make it in the writing world. Right now, I had more important things ahead of me, I had to walk again then, I would try maybe to finish the book as promised.

Chapter 6

The morning came quickly; the sun was shining through my window and directly into my eyes forcing me to wake up earlier than I had planned. I finally had a good night's sleep, without any nightmares. The clock on the stand next to me read seven in the morning, which meant that soon the doctors would be in to prepare me for my first day of therapy. In a way I couldn't wait for it to begin, but in another way I was scared. Usually I had always had someone around me when I was in the state of mind I was in and this time I had to do it alone. It's funny how in certain circumstances in one's life we learn who our friends really are causing us to reevaluate how we perceive things to be. I remember being in a fight one day after school, and all the people I thought were my friends, had finally shown their true colors. That was a day that made me choose my friends more carefully and maybe that's what everyone should learn eventually in their life. Sometimes we all have to learn the hard way about who we can trust, in order to make us a better person. I was about to walk down my own fork in the road, one that I had to chose in order for me to begin my life again. I knew that what lay ahead of me would be a great test of my inner strength, but would later result in the chance to walk to Josh's grave and be able to spend time with him so I could say good bye to my best friend.

As I sat there thinking, A very familiar face happened to poke around the corner into the room, Andy a friend I hadn't seen since the party and began to wonder if he was still my friend. "Can I come in, or is it a bad time?" He asked as he walked in slowly. "What brings you here so early? If the nurses catch you they may ask you to leave, visiting hours aren't till this afternoon." I replied to him. "Yeah I know. They said it would be all right for a short visit. I hear you start therapy this morning, congratulations." Andy said. "I was wondering if I'd see you, or if you'd forgotten me." I answered. "I didn't forget, it's just that I've been busy. I got a new record deal and I owe it all to you." Andy said smiling. "What exactly did I do to help get you the record deal?" I asked. "I didn't know it, but at your party, a big time producer was there and heard me playing and called me the next day and asked if I'd be interested in recording a new album. According to the contract, I'd be making enough money to later open my own recording studio." He said excitedly. "That's great. Just make sure I get the first autographed copy." I replied. I knew one day Andy would get the contract of his dreams. He explained in better detail as to what he would be getting over the next hour as I waited for the doctor. I was friends with a rock star; things just kept getting better. As he was explaining his success, I looked over and saw the copy of the book I had been working on, and wanted the same for me so bad that I could almost taste it.

After what seemed an eternity for me, the doctor poked his head in the room and said that he'd be back in an hour and we'd begin my therapy. "What's wrong, you all right?" He asked as he saw me stop smiling. "It's nothing. I just wish things would be going as good for me with my book. I'm afraid to finish it, but yet I want to so bad." I replied to him. "First things first, you have to get back on your feet so you can get back the confidence you lost in yourself. Then you'll know when it's time to finish the book. Josh and everyone else would tell you to concentrate on what needs to be done first." Andy stated putting his hand on my shoulder. "You've worked very hard and it shows with how much you've gotten done. Be proud of the work you all ready did. I know that when the time comes you'll be able to finish it and it will be a success." He said heading towards the door. "Where you going, you just got here?" I asked him. "I wish I could stay, but you've got a lot of work ahead of you and so do I. I'll be around if you need me, until then I'll see you in a couple of days." Andy said as he headed out the door. Just as he left the doctor came in, almost as though he'd been listening the whole time. "I suppose you listened in on a private conversation?" I said. "You got a lot of people on your side, why don't you talk to them about how you really feel inside?" The doctor replied. "They have no idea what it's like to be like this. How do I even know if I'll ever walk again? What if the therapy fails and I never get to walk again, I'm not sure it's worth the risk." I answered rudely. "So it's the same reason you will not finish writing, your afraid to fail so you figure it'd be best to avoid the pain of trying to win?" The doctor said to me as he held up my book. Failing was all I had done for the past several weeks and it seemed to agree with me, so why not give up.

The pain I felt inside was like a volcano waiting to erupt, the pressure kept building up inside me the same way. The only difference was I was too afraid to hurt anyone else or even burden them with the way I felt inside. "They're your friends, the same as Josh was, let them inside before it's too late for you. I can't force you to go through with the therapy, but I will tell you this, give the therapy a chance." The doctor said. "You didn't even know my friend Josh, what gives you the right to say how he'd feel? I was there the night he died; I did nothing so I am to blame. I'll never know what kind of friend I was to him, I'll never know if we had a real friendship. Everytime I close my eyes, I still see the dead stare in his eyes. Do you realize what that's like; I can't get that picture out of my mind. Sometimes I even hate him for doing what he did, he cheated me out of a friendship that meant everything to me." I yelled in anger. "It's going to hurt for some time, but your not to blame for what happened, inside you know that's true. In time you will learn the truth for yourself." The doctor replied. At that point it was a good thing that I couldn't walk or I would've ran away as fast as I could, hoping to outrun the pain inside. The doctor said he'd give me some time to cool down and that he'd send someone in that may be able to change my mind about a lot of things. Somehow, I didn't think anyone like that existed.

I dozed off for a couple of hours only to be awaken by an unfamiliar voice. "Wake up. Come on it's time to wake up and get ready for your therapy." The voice said. I awoke slowly, my eyes struggling to see the shape of the figure standing above me. "Leave me alone. Just let me sleep, I'm not in the mood for anyone else to deal with." I answered as I tried to fall back asleep. It was only a few moments before I felt the covers ripped off my bed and the person standing above me trying to pull me from the bed. "What's the big idea, don't you realize I can't walk? I demand to talk to someone in charge!" I said trying to push the call button. Before I could push the button, the figure pulled the remote from my hand and yanked the plug from the wall. "I guess you'll have to settle for me, know are you ready to try this again or do I resort to more drastic measures?" The voice said. "Since when are patients treated like this! I demand to talk to your boss, I'll have your ass fired before you know what hit's you." I replied in anger. The mood of the person didn't change, even though I kept on yelling he continued to use more force than I used each time. "I want to be left alone, can't anyone understand I don't deserve a second chance. I failed once, I'll fail again." I answered. The shadow became clearer and still stood over me as though he were the reaper coming to take me away.

We argued back and forth and I realized I wasn't going to win, only because he stood his ground and I couldn't move much at all to defend myself. "We can do this all day, but your going through with the therapy. Its too late to back out now." The voice said. "Why are you doing this to me, I just want to be left alone." I answered. "I was sent by the doctor to assist you while you go through your therapy." He said sitting down on the bed. "I've been through something similar that your going through and I became a volunteer here at the hospital." He said to me. "Who are you anyway? And what did you go through?" I asked. "Sorry, My names Kyle. I too lost a close friend and it hurt for some time. I became suicidal and blamed myself for his death." Kyle said. All this time, I thought I was the only one this ever happened to. "What happened to him?" I asked feeling a little better at ease. "Well, I'll tell you the rest, but first we've got to get you to therapy agreed?" Kyle said lifting me into the chair. I decided to give things a chance and listen to what Kyle had to say who knows maybe I could learn something.

It appeared that I didn't have much of a choice anyway, it seemed to me that he had this planned out from the beginning. I had to give him credit, he had my attention and I did want to know more about his friend. "Do you want to take anything with you, you'll be gone for a few hours?" Kyle asked. "No, I don't think I'll need anything. Are you going to tell me about you and your friend or not?" I replied. "After your therapy session, then we'll go somewhere and talk." Kyle said as he wheeled me out of the room. "I thought I had to see a shrink first?" I asked him. "You were, but the doctor decided to send me instead. He thought that we'd have something in common and that I may be better help to you." He replied. I felt a little relieved that I would be able to talk to someone that knew exactly what I felt. "So exactly what kind of therapy will I be going through?" I asked. "First, I think you'll start with leg lifts, it will hurt at first but eventually you'll gain a little strength so you can hold onto bars and put some weight on you feet." He replied. "Sounds sort of painful, what if I can't do it?" I asked. "It's not like you have to succeed the first time, we'll take as long as necessary in order for you to gain the strength you need." He answered me. Something inside me told me that this wasn't going to be easy.

I knew everyone meant well, and I appreciated all their help, but learning to walk again was something I never thought I'd have to do. I was afraid and I kept thinking that I was wasting my time. It felt awkward, maybe more like I was a helpless child learning to walk for the first time, all I wanted was to be eventually able to put all of this behind me and maybe get on with my life. The days ahead, weren't going to be as easy as I hoped they would be, I guess if we want something bad enough in life we have to work extra hard for it. However, I didn't understand why someone that didn't know me would be so interested in helping me regain what I had lost. I knew he had nothing to gain, and I was at a loss for words for the first time in my life. "So, what else do you do besides help strangers?" I asked him. "Well, I went back to school and got my G.E.D. and I like to read a lot." He replied. "Maybe if I ever finish writing my book, you could read it and let me know what you think of it." I said to him. "You're a writer, that's pretty cool. I never met a writer before. So how's it coming along so far?" He asked. "Actually, I was almost finished when this all started and I hadn't been in the mood to do much writing since." I replied to him. "I'd love to read what you've got so far, if it's all right with you? I promise I will not let anything happen to it and I'll return it as soon as possible." Kyle said. "I'll have to think about that, I guess I'll let you know after the therapy session. It's just that I had hoped that this book would have changed my life and Josh's forever." I answered. "Was he the one that died. I'm really sorry about that and if you want to talk about it let me know I'll be glad to listen. A person shouldn't keep things like that bottled up inside." Kyle said as we entered the therapy room.

We'll, I guess I was about to find out that there was more pain that I would have to go through. The room was filled with weight benches, saunas, free weights and even a small pool. I started to become more afraid when I saw the pool, not being able to swim was bad enough but I couldn't walk and knew I'd drown for sure if I were put inside the pool. "I hope I'm not going into the pool at all, I can't swim." I asked Kyle. "Don't worry, the pool is just to help you loosen up your legs. No one will let you drown. If you want, I'll be right there with you." Kyle replied. I was very afraid of the water; even being unable to walk didn't change that outlook. It's funny how some fears just never go away. "Jim, I'll be with you every step of the way. I'm actually the one that's supposed to help you with all of this, but you have to learn to trust me. Nothing bad is going to happen to you." Kyle said as he knelt down beside the chair. Kyle started to remind me a lot of the way Josh treated me, he was always right there if ever I needed him and maybe it was Josh after all that sent Kyle to help me. Everything about Kyle I knew so far did remind me of Josh, I found that very strange in fact. I had only known Kyle a short time and already I thought I could trust him. I only wish that it were Josh himself that was here. "I think we'll start with some basic leg lifts, I'll help lift your legs and you try to hold them as long as you can." Kyle said raising my legs. The pain itself was intense and I could feel the fact that my legs wanted to just drop, which is exactly what happened.

My legs were like weights; I couldn't find the strength to hold them up, which became very frustrating. As I looked around me I could see I wasn't the only one in the room, there was at least three others beside me, including a teenager a few years younger. I struggled over and over only to fail each time. Kyle just smiled at me and kept encouraging me to not give up, even though it would've been easier to give up. I began to feel like I was getting nowhere. "It's okay, you'll get it eventually. This is the first time so we got all day if you want to." Kyle said without pressuring me. "I hope your right, because this is really starting to make me mad. I didn't think it would be this difficult to do." I replied struggling again. "Let's try something slower, I'll keep lifting your legs and you try to lift with me." Kyle said as he began to lift my legs. I stared at my legs as if willing them to do what I wanted and somehow I managed to hold them up for a short time. "You did it. I knew you could do it." Kyle said. "I barely held them up." I answered. "Come on, be proud of what you did. I never said it would be easy, but it's one hell of a start. Do you want to keep working on it some more?" Kyle asked me. "Could we take a break, I'm sort of tired and I could really use a drink." I said. "Sure, anything you want. I'll be right back I'll get you a soda." Kyle said as he went to the vending machine. I wish I had felt as excited as he did about what little I accomplished.

While I waited for Kyle to come back, I looked at everyone else and saw that they to were struggling to overcome their pain. I noticed Kyle talking to the doctor and couldn't exactly make out what they were saying, but I did see the doctor smile at me. "Hey why so down, You're making progress. You should be glad, this means that things will get better. Each night when your in your room you have to try to move your legs even if only an inch. In time you will walk." Kyle said as he patted me on the shoulder. I looked up at him and saw him smile as he handed me the soda. "Drink this, and if you want to work some more we will." He said to me. I took the soda and drank it slowly; Kyle had bought himself one and sat on the bench beside me drinking his as well. "You said you'd tell me about your friend, are you going to keep your promise?" I asked him. "I didn't lie. I'll tell you everything you want to know, but like I said you have to trust me, or I can't help you." Kyle said taking a sip of his soda. "Deal. Is there anyway we can call it a day?" I asked him. "Sure, is everything all right? I'll keep working with you if you want, I have no plans." Kyle asked me. "Everything's all right, I just feel like a little fresh air if that's allowed?" I answered. "I think that can be arranged. Let's finish our soda and then we'll go outside." Kyle replied. I really needed to get out of the hospital for a little while, everything was so depressing which made me more depressed myself.

Kyle wheeled me to the main lobby and out the doors, I finally felt free even if it was for just a short while. The atmosphere in the hospital was actually starting to get to me and I needed a change of scenery in order to gain my thoughts. It had been a long day, longer than I realized I had been in the therapy room for almost three hours. Time just managed to pass by quickly, even though it felt longer. Kyle wheeled me to the other side of the hospital, which was a small park with trees and benches. There was even a small pond nearby that for the first time I was able to see myself in the reflection of the water. "How about we get you out of that dam chair, I think you'll be more comfortable on the grass." Kyle said as he lifted me without waiting for an answer. "Thanks for your help today." I said as he sat me down. "It's my job, besides it will be worth while eventually, you wait and see." Kyle said. "You have a cigarette, I haven't had one in quite a while and sure could use one." I asked him. "I really shouldn't, but here I'll let you have one. How about putting your feet in the water, you might feel something?" He said. "Okay, I guess it can't hurt." I said. Before I could finish, my feet were all ready in the pond and I could feel how refreshing the water felt. I hadn't been out side so long that I almost forgot what the warm sun felt like. I even forgot how good it felt to be out in the fresh air.

We sat on the wall, I finished my cigarette, and Kyle was on his second soda. "How long were you and Josh friends for, if you don't mind me asking?" He asked. "We knew each other all our lives. We were best friends." I answered trying to hold back the tears. Kyle was looking right at me and knew he had hit a soft spot that I was unable to face without a tear. "I'm sorry, I know how close the two of you were and I know it hurts." Kyle replied putting his hand on my shoulder. "It's okay, Eventually I'll have to face the fact that he's gone. I've never lost anyone before and I never realized how much it hurts." I answered. "I lost my friend a year ago, and it still hurts to this day. The pain never really goes away, but you learn to go on even though it's hard. I miss my friend too." Kyle said in confidence. "Is it me, or is everything you see remind you of what you did together?" I asked him. "It's true, I feel the same way. We did a lot together and every time I pass by the beach I remember how much fun we used to have there growing up." Kyle replied. I couldn't believe I was able to talk to Kyle about Josh, for the longest time I had wanted to talk about how great of a friend he was to me. Kyle was about my age, and had blond hair, from what I knew of him I guess that I could trust him. I had to be able to trust someone again.

The sun was very hot that day, but I didn't mind it at all it really felt nice to be outside the way Josh and I used to spend summer days of the past. Kyle just sat there, willing to listen to anything I had to say and even willing to help me get through with the therapy ahead. Perhaps, Josh sent him and if so it would be something I could never know for sure. Right now, the only thing that did matter was that I felt better than I had in a long time. I didn't want to lose the thoughts I had about Josh, inside he still existed and that's the way I want to be able to keep him alive. I guess as long as we remember the good times we had; a person is never truly gone spiritually. Josh and I had shared a lot of great times together, I miss those days that we spent even more so I missed him. Whenever I was in a bind he was always there to cheer me up or make the day seem better. Often times we just sat and talked, it was good enough for us considering the fact that neither of us had much money to be going out all the time. Here I was sitting with someone that truly reminded me of Josh, hell he was almost like him. I could tell that Kyle was someone I could trust, he wouldn't be here if I couldn't. I still wondered why he would be so willing to help a complete stranger that he hardly knew. I guess I had a lot more to learn about trusting people than I did. "Do you want to stay out here for a while longer or do you want to go inside?" Kyle asked. "Let's just stay a little longer, I haven't been outside in quite awhile and it kind of feels good to get away from the hospital." I answered. To me it felt like I was free, even though I was bound to the chair temporarily. I reached inside my shirt and pulled out the chain and held onto it tightly and closed my eyes to see the eagle flying through the clouds.

As I sat there I could feel the wind blowing across my face the cool air was like the open sea and I imagined that I was there, for the first time in a while my only thoughts were of being free from that which held me back. I knew then that I had to break the chains that wanted to keep me from fulfilling a dream that I had within me. Josh had told me that I was a great writer, and I finally saw that he was right. First, I had to learn to walk again, and then I had to finish what I started for the both of us. "You okay? You look like you've seen a ghost." Kyle asked concerned. "I'm fine. I finally see what everyone's trying to show me and I know now that they're right." I replied. "Congratulations, That's the first step to the road for recovery. I knew you'd find it in time. If you want me to continue helping you just say so, or I can get someone else to help you." Kyle said. "No, I think you're the one who's supposed to help me. I know it sounds weird, but I think Josh sent you to help me regain what I had lost." I answered. "That doesn't really sound weird, maybe your right. Strange things happen in life and maybe we can help each other overcome our losses." Kyle replied relieved. They say good things come to those who wait, maybe that saying was in fact the one that I'd been waiting for. Maybe Kyle was sent, maybe he wasn't, the only thing that mattered now was that he was here to help and I knew I should accept.

Kyle picked me up and put me back in the chair, and knelt down beside me and undid the brakes. "You know, it's going to be all right in time. Everything will work out if you let time take its course. I'd like to be around if you let me, I think this could be the start of a great friendship." He said as he stood up. I wanted to be friends, but inside I felt as though the same thing would happen to me all over again. What I mean, is I was afraid to lose another friend by either a fight, or moving away. Maybe that was just an excuse or maybe an actual fear; I wasn't exactly sure what it was at the time. I even felt that maybe the timing wasn't right. I knew that Kyle did in fact mean well and maybe he was sincere but it was me that was scared. I knew this was something I'd have to think about seriously and consider if I was to ever take a chance like that again in my life.

The sun started to go down, I guess we stayed outside longer than we expected to. It was just too perfect a day to stay inside not to mention we got to talking and getting to know each other which time often moves faster than one can keep up with. As we headed inside my stomach began to rumble I hadn't had anything to eat all day and was starving. "How about we go out and get something to eat, my treat we'll call it a celebration for your progress." Kyle said. "If you're buying, then let's go for it. Only one thing, I didn't think I could leave the grounds?" I said to him excitedly. "You're not, but who said anyone has to know. We'll sneak out on the town and be back before anyone knows you're gone. I'm the one that will get in trouble not you so don't worry." Kyle replied. "Okay, but I really don't want you to lose your job for something stupid." I said to him. "I'll worry about that, besides you need to get away for awhile." Kyle answered. With that we head back to the room to make it appear that I was still there, it became sort of like the thing you do when your young and sneak out of the house at night. We put pillows in the bed and covered them up and put a do not disturb sign on the door to cover our tracks. The nurses station was not even aware of the fact that we sneaked right passed them. The game was afoot and our adventure into the great unknown was about to begin. I was so anxious to get out; I almost burst out screaming for joy at my escape.

Once we cleared the lobby, it was easy the rest of the way. All we had to do was go to the parking lot and drive off; no one knew a thing. Or so I thought, the doctor was still in his office and had heard the doors close and looked out the window and smiled. I didn't realize it until we came back later that Kyle and the doctor had planned it. "Okay let's get you inside, then we'll decide where to go to eat. This is something I haven't done since I was real young to go to a party." Kyle laughed as he put me in the car. The car was a mustang, real nice interior and plenty of room for a wheel chair. "If it's all right, could we go through drive through. I really feel embarrassed about being seen in a wheel chair." I asked him as we drove off. "No problem. I know exactly where we can go to eat. Maybe we can talk some more, I mean if you want to." Kyle said to me. I just sat there for a moment relaxing and enjoying the fact that I was away from that hospital for the first time in a long time. "How about some music, I haven't really listened to the radio in a while." I asked. "Sure, go right ahead and turn it on if you want. I got a great sound system in here I'm sure you'll like it." Kyle replied. I turned the radio on to a station of calm, mellow music with a bit of soul. Something I really needed right now.

We pulled into the burger joint and I could smell the food from the parking lot. "I hope you don't get in trouble over all your doing for me. I really appreciate the chance you're taking." I said to him as we pulled up to the window. "Like I said, don't worry. Now what would you like?" Kyle asked. "Just a couple of burgers and a fry, and a medium drink." I answered. "Are you sure that's all you want, You can order more if you're hungry?" Kyle asked as we pulled up. "No, I'm sure. Just the idea of eating fast food again is great." I replied. Kyle pulled up to the window and ordered our dinner, me I just sat there looking around at all the people hanging out with their friends. The parking lot was full which meant that most of the high school students were here and I hoped not to run into too many people I really didn't want anyone to see me this way until I could stand on my own two feet. I missed hanging out with my friends, the way Josh and I used to do. We had so many good times doing that and I longed for the day I would be able to do it again. Kyle pulled up to the pick up window and paid for the food and we took our order and pulled into the parking lot. "How about we go to my place and eat, I promise no one there will bother you. After that I'll take you back to the hospital, if you want." Kyle said. "I thought I had no choice but to go back tonight. What exactly are you up to? I don't really know you and you don't really know me, so why are doing all this?" I asked him. "You're right, I planned all this to get you out for the night. I thought it would help you to see the world going on around you and that it would convince you to work hard to walk again. I also hoped we could be friends, I figure we have a lot in common and we could learn from each other. I want to give it a chance, How about you?" Kyle said as we headed to his house. I was a bit surprised that someone that hardly knew me would want to be a friend to me. I wasn't sure I was ready to make any new friends right now. "I guess I'm staying at your house then. I'm still not convinced we can be friends, but I'll give it a shot." I replied to him.

I couldn't believe that I had been tricked, I actually thought that Kyle would get into trouble for taking me from the hospital. I never thought for a moment that it did seem to easy for us to sneak out of the hospital without being seen. I figured the doctor also had to be in on it and started to laugh out loud as we drove away. "What's so funny?" Kyle asked. "I can't believe you did this, I was trying not to get caught and all the while you had it all planned." I said laughing. "We'll then, don't you think it's time for you to enjoy yourself a little? I guarantee that you'll be able to relax and enjoy your night away. If you want to talk, we can talk. You decide as the night goes on." Kyle said as we pulled down the road to his house. The night was young and we had a lot of time ahead of us and I couldn't wait to get inside and eat. Kyle lived in a big house, with a large yard. It was still early as we arrived and I looked at the doorway and saw how small it was. I wasn't sure the wheel chair would fit through the door, and I also saw that the stairs leading to the door were steep. "How do you think I'll get inside, look at the stairs and the door? Maybe this wasn't a good idea." I asked. "First, don't worry about a thing. I'll carry you inside and then I'll get the chair for you. The inside is bigger than it looks." Kyle addressed me. "You're going to carry me in? Why do you care so much about helping me? Why waste your time on someone like me?" I asked him. "You have to learn to go with the flow and accept someone else's help once in a while. You can trust me; I'm not about to let anything happen to you. Just lighten up a little." Kyle said as he got out of the car.

As Kyle went to open the door, I felt somewhat awkward about intruding on his family and the thought of being seen by them in a wheel chair was somewhat embarrassing. I watched Kyle as he came over to the passenger side door and unlocked the back and took the chair inside. It was something that Josh would've done as well; he'd always help out friend no matter what it was. "I'll be back to get you in just a minute." Kyle said as he went inside with the chair. For the life of me, I couldn't believe a total stranger would let someone he hardly knew into his home the way Kyle was doing right this minute. Night had began to fall and I was getting really tired, but I forced myself to try to stay awake, I didn't want to ruin my first night out that I had in a long time. I sat there thinking as to how Kyle intended on getting me into the house without me having access to my chair. As he returned, he opened the passenger side door and picked me up like I was a sack of potatoes. I never felt so embarrassed as I did just then. "Wouldn't it be easier if you 'd left the chair? At least then you wouldn't throw out your back." I asked him as we walked to the door.

"Don't worry about me, I've carried many patients and haven't had a problem at all." Kyle replied. At that point, I couldn't wait to walk again and even looked forward to more therapy as they called it, but I called it pain 101.

I couldn't help but look around once we were inside, his house was enormous I couldn't believe the size of the hallway itself. The hall must have been at least the size of two rooms. "I forgot to tell you, we also have a hot tub, which might be good to help get the circulation back in your legs. Maybe after an hour or so of sitting in there, you can try some of your exercises. I'll even help you." Kyle said as he put me in my chair. From where I was sitting, everything around me looked so huge compared to the way I was used to seeing things. Even my new friend seemed taller than he actually was. I understood how people confined to a wheel chair must feel. I was hopefully going to be lucky enough to walk again and looked forward to that day that lay ahead of me. "So, how about we get you settled in, then we can decide what to do?" Kyle said to me as he wheeled me into the parlor. "I hope this isn't putting anyone out, I really don't want to get in the way." I said as he fixed the couch for me to sleep on. "I told you, it's no problem. We've got plenty of room and I think you could use the time away from the hospital." Kyle said. "Where are you going to sleep?" I asked not wanting to be alone. "I'll take the other couch, that way if you need anything during the night you can wake me." Kyle said as he sat down on the couch next to the one he fixed for me. I could tell that this was going to be a great night like he said it was to be.

The parlor had three couches and even a pool table, which was unusual for a room like this. I never expected to see a pool table inside a parlor before. Kyle noticed I was looking around and didn't seem to mind that I was getting a feel for the room around me. The last thing I wanted was to hit anything as I wheeled myself around the room. It felt nice to have someone looking out for me for a change. "Well, what would you like to do first, you name it and we'll do it?" Kyle asked. "How about we go into the hot tub, I could really get used to that. I've never really been in one before and I'm kind of looking forward to trying it out." I said to Kyle. I figured if I was going to relax, why not do it in style. "No problem, I brought a pair of shorts for you and I'll go and change myself and be right back. Can you manage on your own?" Kyle asked. "Yeah I can change, but I'll need some help getting in if you don't mind." I said as he headed up to his room. "I would hope you wouldn't try getting in by yourself, I'll be right back and I'll put you in." Kyle said to me. After Kyle went upstairs, I changed as quickly as I could and waited for him to return. I wheeled myself around the room and noticed that Kyle had won many awards for community service, which made me feel more secure around him. I realized he must know exactly what he's doing.

A short time later, Kyle came down the stairs already for the hot tub, I of course was more than anxious to get in and relax. I wheeled myself, as close as I could get so Kyle wouldn't have to carry me as far. "In a hurry I see, that's great. I'm sure this will help you a great deal, so just sit back and relax once we're inside." Kyle said as he lifted me out of the chair. The temperature read a hundred and seven degrees, which was very warm but also very normal for a hot tub to be. Kyle lifted me over the railing and sat me down inside. Once my body hit the water, I could feel the difference in temperature. The water wasn't nearly as bad as I thought it was going to be. It felt nice and relaxing just sitting there. Kyle entered soon after and we both just sat there relaxing before even speaking. I couldn't believe how great the water felt and how comfortable I actually felt. I felt as if the rest of the world didn't even exist. "How do you like it?" Kyle asked me. "I could sit here for hours, it's incredible I've never felt so relaxed before." I replied. "Yeah, that's definitely one of the great perks of having a hot tub." He said as he rested his head on the back of the tub. Kyle told me that the water temperature might help my muscles to relax enough so it would make the exercises easier. He also said that it wouldn't be as painful trying to stretch them out. I figured he knew what he was doing and decided to let him do what he felt was right.

Sitting in the water my body felt as though it was floating on air, I could actually feel the water relaxing my muscles and knew that it was working. I started to get some feeling in my legs, at first a sharp pain then my legs moved as though some outside force controlled them. "Kyle, my legs I got some feeling back in them." I said excitedly. "Are you sure it was you and not the water moving them?" Kyle questioned. I knew he needed to know if it was I or the water causing them to move. "It was me, look I can move my ankle around a little bit. I can't believe this the water is relaxing me." I said as I tried harder to move my legs. Kyle watched as my legs did move, not as much as I wanted them to but it was a start. "We'll sit in here for awhile longer, then we can work on some of your exercises and see what happens. Don't get frustrated, it's definitely a good start and it shows there is hope for you to walk soon." Kyle replied. I sat there thinking about walking again. The thought was overwhelming and I owed it all to someone I hardly knew. If Kyle wouldn't have been so persistent in trying to help me, I may have given up on walking again." I thought to myself. I was always one for giving up on myself and relied on others to convince me otherwise that I can do it if I was willing to fight for what I desired. Although sometimes the odds are against you, as long as you try, the outcome is usually worth the effort to fight.

Kyle just sat there relaxing, it was as though he wasn't going to let anything bother him. The water felt so great that I couldn't help but enjoy myself as well. I'd never felt so relaxed in my life. We must have sat there for at least an hour before either one of us spoke. I didn't realize the time had flown by so fast. We decided that we'd better get started on my exercises. Kyle lifted me out and put me in my chair and I dried myself off. I didn't notice it before now that Kyle had a very large scar on his abdomen. "How'd you get that scar?" I asked him. Kyle looked down at it before he even spoke. "I was stabbed a couple of years ago, and a friend found me and saved my life. If it weren't for him being close by, I would have bled to death." Kyle answered. Kyle finished drying off and pushed me into the living room so we'd have more room to work. He put me close enough to the couch that I decided it was time for me to try to get out of the chair on my own instead of relying on others to help me. "You sure you don't need any help?" Kyle asked as I forced my upper body onto the couch. "Thanks, but if I don't start trying on my own I'll never do it." I answered as I lifted my legs out of the chair and onto the couch. "Congratulations, you did it. Your upper body is gaining strength, now let's see if we can get your legs to do the same." Kyle replied. I breathed a sigh of relief, I thought for sure I'd fall on my ass. One step at a time was all I kept saying to myself as I got comfortable and waited for Kyle to begin the exercises that hopefully would put me on the right path to recovery.

Kyle began the exercises by placing my foot against his hand and straightening my leg and then bending it as far as he could back towards me, at first it was a bit painful as I could feel my muscles stretching. I was flat on my back and I began to have slight feeling in my legs. He continued with the same exercise on both legs for at least an hour. I felt as though I was riding a bike. It was like I was peddling fast and getting no where. Kyle stopped suddenly, which was a relief because my back was sore from being in the same position for so long. "I got to sit up for a minute, my back is stiff." I said as he helped me sit up. "I need a break myself, next I want you to try to push against my hand as hard as you can. It may take a while before you can move it but try." Kyle said as he sat back. I sat there daydreaming about being able to walk again, I dreamed of how great it was to run and how much I had missed it. I guess we take advantage of the things we have in life without thinking in a split second they could all be gone forever. In my case however, I had a chance, a chance that few people would ever have and at first I was willing to throw it all away for self-pity. Josh wouldn't want me to give up and I finally realized I shouldn't give up either. Had Josh been here, he would have been on my case just as much as Kyle was and I had to try for that reason alone.

Josh would be turning over in his grave if he had known that I even thought of giving up. The idea of Josh screaming and yelling at me was one thought I could live without, so I knew what I had to do. I may not have Josh to help me through this, but at least I had Kyle and he wasn't about to give up on me either. It was however like having Josh here to help guide me after all. Kyle I noticed was a lot like him, they both had the attitude to fight on even though the odds weren't that great. At first I hadn't seen that in Kyle but later I began to notice how strong willed he was. Somebody had to keep my ass in gear because I sure wasn't ready to be alone again, and I knew I never would be alone as long as Kyle was around. I couldn't believe I had let my own life get so out of control, I literally let myself fall apart without thinking. I knew it was normal to grieve hard for a loss of a friend, but I had not thought about anyone else but myself and that was wrong. I should have tried to keep his memory alive that's how you remember someone close to you. "Well, are you ready to try again?" Kyle said interrupting my thoughts. No pain, no gain I thought to myself as I nodded my head yes.

Before we could even start, Kyle's mom and dad came in from the other room. "How's the patient doing Kyle?" His dad asked. "We seem to be making good progress so far, would you care to sit in and see what happens?" Kyle asked. "No, I think your mother and I might make him feel a little nervous. We just thought we'd come in and see how things were going and to see if the two of you would like something to eat. I'll get take out for you both and have it delivered." His dad asked. "Sounds great, I guess we could use a pizza. I know I'm hungry again. We still have a lot of work ahead of us but it will pay off eventually." Kyle replied. "I don't think we've formally met your friend, I'm Kyle's dad and this is his mom." His father answered reaching out his hand. "Nice to meet you both, my name's Jim. Kyle's doing a great job helping me out like this and I really appreciate it a lot." I said shaking his dad's hand. "Well, I'll order the pizza and we'll be leaving you two to you're work. If you need anything just yell. It was nice to meet you Jim good luck." His dad said leaving the room. "You're parents are pretty cool, They must really trust you." I said. "Yeah, they are cool. My father's a pretty good teacher when it comes right down to it. My dad teaches a course on therapy at the local college. He taught me a few things and I want to become a therapist as well." Kyle said. "Well I'll give you that, It's a worthy profession to get into. I'm sure you'll do great." I said. "I hope so, you're my first real patient I get to work with. You might say my first test subject." Kyle said laughing. "That makes me feel a lot better. Just don't twist anything that don't need to be rearranged, do we have a deal?" I said joking. "No promises, hell I make mistakes too." Kyle said laughing.

A short time later, the pizza arrived and we decided to take a break and eat. Even though I didn't have much money with me, I paid for the pizza it was the least I could do for all the help that Kyle was giving me. As we ate, we shared some laughs and had a great time, something I needed very much in my life. I hadn't really enjoyed myself since Josh died and a part of me felt guilty for having fun without him. "What's wrong?" Kyle asked. "I feel a little guilty about having fun without Josh. We did everything together." I answered. "Don't worry about it, it's normal to feel that way. But you do have to get on with your life, Josh wouldn't want you to give up on your dreams." Kyle replied burning his mouth. It did seem weird not sharing things with him, the way we used too. "It's okay to miss someone, but if you live in the past too much it can hurt your future. I'm sure the two of you had a lot of great time and you shouldn't forget any of them, that's what you can do to keep Josh alive." Kyle said. At about the time he finished talking, something unexpected happened, I began to get feeling back in my legs at first a sharp pain then just numbness. I knew then that it was a sure sign of the days ahead that walking again was a reality. Kyle could tell by the look in my eyes that I felt my legs he wasted no time in saying that we should continue a little more on the exercises in order to cash in on the opportunity that was received. “That means your leg muscles are getting better, This time it will hurt more but you have to fight the pain and take it.” Kyle said as he continued bending my legs slowly. At that point, I knew what a pretzel felt like. I was being bent in all directions and I didn’t know the human body was capable of being placed in those positions.

Kyle was right; the pain was more intense than ever before. I wasn’t sure how to react, in a way I wanted to stop but if I did I knew that all would be in vain. While I questioned giving up, Kyle wasn’t about to let that happen. He kept on forcing my muscles to move, it was as though failure didn’t exist at all for him. Finally, I had to stop. I wanted to keep going but the pain was so intense that I felt as though my legs were going to fall off. “Let’s stop, my legs are sore. WE can do more when we’re back at the hospital.” I said. Kyle agreed and we just sat there for a time realizing how late it was. "Would you like to try standing on them, you might be able to put some weight on them for sure now.” Kyle said as he reached out his hand. “I guess I don’t have much of a choice do I?” I said as I took his hand. “Pull yourself up, just use me as support for your weight in case you fall. If I stand you it will do no good, you have to be the one to do this."” Kyle said as he stood there. I did as he said and tried to pull my self of the couch and stand. At first I couldn’t do it, but on the second try I managed to stand for a very short time before falling on the floor. “Sorry about that, but you did it. You actually stood up for a short time. I think that’s worth everything we did today.” Kyle replied as he helped me up. He was right, I shouldn’t give up on walking again.

Quitting was always the easy way out for me, I figured that if the pressure was to much I could always give up and try something else even though I eventually quit that too. I guess when some of us become afraid we give up on life’s challenges to easy, even too soon. I knew Kyle wasn’t going to give up on me and I wasn’t about to at this point either. If everyone gave up on life’s challenges, man would never accomplish anything in life. Sometimes no matter how much the odds are against you, you just got to keep fighting in order to win.

After the long battle to stand, Kyle and I just sat there for a time reflecting on my success at standing for such a short time. I was excited at the idea of walking very soon. "It won't be long before you will stand on your own two feet again. In the mean time, let's just relax for the remainder of the night." Kyle said sitting back in the chair. "Do you have a lot of friends?" I asked abruptly. Kyle looked at me before answering. "No, right now I have none at all. Why do you ask?" Kyle replied. "Since Josh died, I didn't realize how close of friends we were. Now that he's gone, I feel pretty empty like I'm all alone. I mean I got other friends but Josh and I did everything together, he pretty much lived at my house. It really hurts." I said. "I understand what you're saying. It's like a part of you died too and you feel the wound may never heal. I've felt the same way you do, I guess I still do." Kyle said. "Then what I need to now is how do I go on, does it get any better or will I always feel that way." I asked him. "The answer sadly, is no it doesn't go away but eventually you learn to deal with it. I miss my friend too and I always think about the fun we had and wish I could do things like that again with him." Kyle replied. "I blamed my self when he died, I feel as though it's my fault he's dead. That night he tried to talk to me but I didn't take him seriously and he went out, the next morning I found him dead in the bathroom and that's when I fell apart." I said to him with my head down in shame. "You can't really blame yourself, I know it feels like you did nothing to help but its just not you're fault." Kyle answered. I just wanted things to make sense and at that point I was still without any answers.

Kyle was easy to talk to, just like Josh was when we sat up all those nights just talking about life ahead of us. I still remember those nights like they were yesterday. I still longed for the chance to have those nights forever. I guess Kyle understood what I was going through and how much it really hurt me, because he never judged me about how much my friend meant to me. "My friend meant as much too me as yours did, and I do know how much it hurts inside to lose someone close to you. I also now how hard it will be to make another friend without thinking that one day you'll lose that friend somehow, maybe that's why I haven't made any new friends since I lost my best friend." Kyle lectured me. "What are trying to say?" I asked. Kyle sat forward in his chair and took a deep breath and relaxed before speaking. "I guess what I'm trying to say is how about we be friends. We both have a lot in common and maybe it's time we both start to get on with our lives. Neither one of us can take the place of the others friends, but at least we could be there for each other when needed." Kyle said. "I'd like that. I can't promise I'll be easy to get along with too soon because I did just lose him. I still need time to deal with everything." I said reaching out my hand in friendship. Kyle reached out his hand and we both made a pact to grow as friends over time.

I never thought after losing my best friend that I'd make a new friend so soon. I could see in Kyle's eyes that he felt the same way. I knew it would take time before we could ever have the friendship that both of us had with our lost friends, but eventually I knew it would pay off in the end. "Did you ever hate Josh for anything he did wrong before?" Kyle asked with hesitation in his voice. "Yeah, there was a particular incident that he made me mad. It was a weekend that we planned on staying at my house and just hanging out and watching movies, playing cards and even drinking in my room. Well, I waited for two hours and he never showed up or called so I called him only to find out he was going away for that weekend with his other friends, I wasn't invited." I started to say. "Then what happened?" Kyle asked. "Well, we ended up in a fight, a fist fight to be exact. That was the first time Josh and I ever hit each other and said things we didn't really mean. I felt like he totally forgot about our plans on purpose." I said. "That must have really hurt. So what happened next?" Kyle said adjusting himself in the chair. "We didn't talk for days, I think neither of us knew what to say. Eventually he showed up at my door and apologized for what happened. He ended up staying over night and getting in trouble with his parents for not calling just to make it up to me. That's when I realized that sometimes plans do change without notice but that doesn't mean our friendship changes." I answered. "At least things worked out for you in the end." Kyle said to me. "I too was ready to apologize to him, but he made the first move. We never fought after that, we always talked out our differences to avoid a conflict like the one we had." I finally said. Talking about those memories made me remember all the good times we had together, all of which could never be replaced.

CHAPTER 7

We talked for what seemed like hours, about the great times we spent with our friends. It seemed that Kyle and his friend had done much the same as Josh and I had done. "I guess we did a lot together over the years. But it feels like everything went by so fast. I always looked forward to what we'd be doing the next day, I never realized that in a split second it could all be gone." I said. "I know what you mean, I've felt the same way too, it's like you want the fun to last forever." Kyle answered. "Did you feel like you were alone after your friend died?" I asked him. "Yeah I did, that's when I decided to start working to try to avoid the feeling of being alone. It doesn't really change things though. I always felt alone even though I was working. I watched as people came in to the hospital with their friends and it reminded me of what I had lost myself." Kyle replied. Loneliness seems to be something that no one can really avoid; it's always there waiting for the right moment to strike anyone. How people deal with it depends on the person, some can deal with it while others can't. The pain I realized would last a lifetime, but I never had to forget about the one best friend that I ever met.

It started to get real late, I guess time does go by quickly when your not paying attention. I had a great time getting things out, being able to talk openly to someone. I figured it did us both some good to talk, we both could go on and on about what we did with our friends but we knew that there would always be time for that later. I was due back at the hospital for my therapy in the morning, even though it was one in the morning already. "Jim, don't you think you should finish your book soon. I mean you're so close to being done that it seems like a waste to just leave it unfinished." Kyle asked me. "I want to, but I'm afraid it won't be any good. What if I finish it and no one will publish it. I just don't think I can deal with the rejection." I answered. "Don't be so hard on yourself, I read what you have done so far, and I like it. Think about the positive side, what if it does sell. You stand to make a lot of money, your every dream could come true." Kyle said. "Josh said the same thing to me. He read it too and said that I should take that chance. I'll have to think about it some more." I replied. With that, I rolled over and fell asleep.

That night, I dreamed about what would come of me being a writer. I would have everything I'd ever wanted in life. The freedom of writing full time and creating a story that people would really enjoy reading and may in fact be able to relate to. Many people called me the word man in high school; maybe it was my destiny to become a writer. It would also be a great way to keep a friend's memory alive. Writing was the only thing that I could see myself doing, it was afterall my gift.

The morning came quickly, the sun glared through the window into my eyes. As I awoke, I looked over to see Kyle was already up sitting in the chair beside me. "Good morning, did you sleep well?" Kyle asked. "Yeah, thanks. How long have you been up for?" I asked him trying to sit up. "About an hour, I just figured I'd let you get some extra sleep before we head back to the hospital." Kyle replied. "I was thinking, do you really think my book is worth finishing?" I asked him. "It really doesn't matter what I think, but yes you should finish it and send it in." Kyle said. Kyle handed me a cigarette and I lit it and just sat back and relaxed before saying another word. I wanted to think really hard about the next biggest decision that I had to make in my life, knowing full well that if I did succeed that it would change my life forever. I was afraid that I would forget how I got to that point in my life, afraid that I'd forget about how Josh helped me as well as how Kyle too had helped to change my life for the better. There was a lot to consider and it was a decision that I had to make carefully. Everything depended on it. "I'll make you a deal." I started to say. "What kind of a deal?" Kyle asked. "I'll finish the book, only if you promise to help me with my exercises so that I can walk again. I don't want to be alone anymore I need a new friend that will always help me when I need it." I stated to him. "You got yourself a deal." Kyle replied reaching out his hand to shake on it. I shook his hand in agreement and that was the start of our pact. With that, I finished my cigarette and Kyle and I decided to head back to the hospital.

As we were driving, Kyle handed me the book I had been working on. I began to feel as the world around me had somehow changed over night. I saw things differently as we drove back to the hospital, I also felt different. I felt like I was ready to take on the world and everything it had to throw at me. Nothing was going to stop me from reaching a goal that I had worked hard for, not even any small set back. "We'll work harder at your therapy from now on, remember no pain no gain." Kyle said with a devious look in his eyes. Some how that look made me nervous, I knew Kyle was going to go to all lengths necessary in order to fullfill his part of the bargain. It also meant that I was in for more pain than before, but this time the outcome was going to be worth the pain I was in for. A promise is a promise no matter what it takes in order to achieve the goal to be reached.

We pulled into the hospital parking lot and parked farther away from the entrance than before. Kyle wasn't about to make this easy for me, if he did I'd get nowhere fast. I needed to get around by myself, or at least try. The time for depending on people was over I had to do this on my own. As I opened the car door, I saw Kyle standing at a distance I knew he wasn't about to help me unless I absolutely needed it. I reached behind the seat to get the chair out and put it beside me and forced my self into the chair and began to wheel myself into the hospital for the long torture that await me. Kyle walked close by careful not to get in my way in case I accidentally ran his feet over as I struggled to make my way into the main lobby of the hospital. Once inside, We made our way over to the desk and Kyle checked me back in. I sat there nervous yet excited at all that I had accomplished. I even looked forward to walking with my new friend instead of wheeling myself around. The hospital itself seemed to look different since the day before, maybe because my hate had been changed into a positive outlook for my future.

I realized that the time ahead would prove to be a real fight to win and this time I was fully prepared to win the battle that lay ahead. Walking was the only thing on my mind at that time. Kyle came back over to me and just looked at me and he decided he wanted to wheel me back upstairs for the last time. "The pain will still be there, that won't change just try to block it out or use it to your advantage to fight harder. I'm not going to leave the room, as a matter of fact I have full permission to continue working with you if you want me to help you the rest of the way." Kyle said as he leaned down beside me in the chair. Without Kyle convincing me to do this, I wouldn't be going through with it and I wasn't about to let him off that easy either. "We have a deal remember, that means you have to stick this out as well. You're not getting off that easy either. So yes, I still need your help or we quit now!" I said to him grabbing his shirt tightly. "Well, at least your upper strength is still there, so what do you say we get started?" He said. "Let's go back to my room first so I can put my stuff away then we'll head back down to the therapy room and get started." I said. "Okay, you should change into you're bathing suit so we can try the pool first." Kyle said smiling knowing full well that I hated the idea of being in a pool. I guess I had no other choice, Kyle did mention that it would be easier to do the exercises in the water to start with.

As Kyle unpacked my things, I went to change into my bathing suit and could almost feel the blood pulsing through my legs. The very thought of walking again sent a nervous feeling into my body, though I knew I wouldn't walk in a day's time I still needed a lot of work. At least this time I was ready for what was ahead of me and I was willing to meet that challenge not alone but with a friend again. I also knew I wouldn't give up on what I wanted any more. Failure was not an option any more in my life, only success was to be my driving factor. I wheeled myself out and saw Kyle sitting on the bed waiting for me. "You ready for this session? We'll stop when you're ready to stop just say the word. We have as long as it takes to get you back on your feet." He said to me. "Let's go. The sooner we get started the better." I answered. We headed downstairs to the therapy room at around eleven in the morning. Once inside the room wasn't that busy most everyone had already been in for their session so Kyle and I had the room mostly to our selves.

We made our way to the pool and as we got closer I started to get a little more nervous and slowed down, Kyle however noticed and pushed the chair forward even though I was fearful of the water and how deep it was. "There's nothing to be afraid of, I won't let you drown. I've even got a life jacket for you to wear while you're inside, and I'll be right inside with you." Kyle said reassuring me. Kyle threw me the life jacket and I put it on slowly while Kyle dove into the pool. "Come on in the waters great." He said as he came up shaking the water off his hair. "How do you expect me to get in on my own?" I said. "We agreed that you'd have to figure things out on your own, remember? First, wheel yourself to the edge of the pool and trust me. Then, when I count to three push your self into the water, the life jacket will help you float back up. I promise you'll float back up there's no way you're going to sink. You have to trust me this time." Kyle said. I sat there on the edge afraid still that I would drown, after all he was asking me to fall into the pool. “Don’t make me get out and throw you in, I really don’t think you’ll enjoy that to much. Just trust me on this, it will help break your fear of the water as well.” Kyle replied. I knew he meant what he said and at that moment remembered watching how Josh dove off a cliff and into the lake below and he came to the surface himself and was fine. I figured maybe Josh gave me that memory right then so I could trust Kyle enough to do what he asked of me. I took a deep breath and decided to give it a shot and pushed myself into the water. While I was briefly under water I could almost feel what Josh must have felt when he dove off that cliff and the sensation rushed through me like I was reborn, It felt incredible. I floated back to the surface as he said I would and was floating. I didn’t feel afraid anymore. “Great job, I told you that you could do it didn’t I?” Kyle said as he swam over to me.

It was a great feeling like a rush of adrenaline that seemed to over take my fears and put them aside. “Now that you’re in, I’m going to rest my hand on your ankle and I want you to try to move your legs, try to force them to move.” Kyle said. I concentrated on moving my legs and felt the muscles begin to respond to my inner thoughts and slowly move. I couldn’t believe I was finally moving them even if it was only slightly. “I did it, I actually moved them.” I said excitedly. “I knew you could do it. Now, let’s try something different. I’ll hold you up and you try to move your feet themselves as if you were swimming.” Kyle said. That task proved not so successful. We continued to try different things for hours, some with success while still other tasks without any success at all. I began to get frustrated and asked if we could try something else outside the water after a break. I couldn’t sit in the water any longer it was starting to get to me and I think that may have been why my success wasn’t as good as it was in the beginning. “Yeah, I guess we could use a break. I’ll help you to the stairs and we can get out and dry off.” Kyle said as he pulled me along like a piece of wood.

Once out of the pool we dried off and sat down to relax for a short while. Kyle looked as though he was impressed with the fact that I finally broke my fear of the water. “How’d it feel, to fall in?” He asked. “I was still scarred up until I came to the surface like you said I would. After that I felt a little more at ease I guess.” I answered. “What made you finally push yourself that extra mile to get in?” Kyle asked. "A few months before Josh died, on his birthday as a matter of fact, Josh wanted to go cliff diving for his birthday and I went with him. I watched as he climbed the cliffs and made his way to the top. He waved from up above and I couldn't believe he had the guts to do it, but he dove off into the water below. He said it was the greatest rush he ever felt in his life…" I replied. "He must have had a great birthday, you're lucky to have shared that with him because you did the same thing by trusting the two of us." Kyle said throwing the towel at me and laughing. "He had a great birthday and yes I was lucky to have that memory with him and to be there to see him do it." I answered. Josh always liked to be a daredevil and maybe that's why he did all those crazy stunts he did.

I actually felt great after that work out, my legs were beginning to show signs of getting stronger and I didn't want to give up to soon. I wanted to at least be able to be on crutches and out of this chair that had become my prison for so long. I sat there quiet for sometime, just thinking about the walking and being able to do the things I used to do. I missed being able to do what I wanted when I wanted. I never realized that walking had now become the greatest obsession in my life. "How about we go back to your room and play some cards for a while? I'll have some lunch sent up and we can just relax before your next session." Kyle asked. "Sure, but first I need a cigarette is it alright if we go outside before we go up?" I replied. "I don't see that as being a problem. I'll get our jackets and were off." Kyle said. I started to enjoy the outdoors more and more; something that I had never been much interested in before. "Josh was the one that influenced me in my writing, he is the person I based my character on. I lost that confidence in myself when I lost him. I was so close to finishing my work and now I don't know how to finish it without his presence." I said abruptly. "With all the memories you have, you should have enough to be able to use. Maybe if you wrote some real events the two of you had you could finish the book and pay tribute to him. I don't think Josh would mind very much, besides everyone that reads it would be able to relate to your characters more themselves." Kyle replied. "I know if I finish it, my writing career may take off real well. I want to write about everything I've seen and done, I just don't know if it's right." I said taking a drag of my cigarette. "All writers need to use what's inside them and what's around them, that's how they tell a great story. My advice is use that talent and stop being so hard on yourself. Finish the book and see what happens, take that chance in your life." Kyle stated.

I felt like I was working against time and I couldn't win. I knew that being a writer wouldn't be easy, but if I had that one chance of success it would change my life. "Think about all that you'd be throwing away if you don't try, the money, a career, being an author, even making your dreams come true. Is it all worth it just to give up? You have a talent that few people have I say use it and use it well." Kyle said with confidence in his voice. We started to go inside when Kyle handed me the book I was writing. He said nothing; instead he just looked at me as though he himself knew my own future better than I did at that moment. "You have that much confidence in me?" I asked. "Yeah I do. Think of it setting your own hours, your time will be yours and you'll never have to punch a clock again." Kyle said pushing me to the elevator. That would be great, working when I wanted to my time belonging to me. That sounded so great. Our paths we take in life were forever changing, perhaps to offer new challenges to see if we made the right choices in our own lives.

When we got back to my room, I put the book on the stand beside the bed and reached inside the draw for the cards. I wasn't the greatest card player, but I did manage to win a few hands by dumb luck. "I think tomorrow we'll start working on the weights to get your leg strength back. If all goes well, you can even try to stand on your feet again. The more you work at it the faster it will come that you will take small steps." Kyle said as he beat my hand in cards again. Our lunch arrived just in time to save me from losing another game; he'd only won the last five out of fifteen. We didn't talk much as we ate, I guess people run out of things to say after a while. I was getting some feeling back in my legs so I knew the therapy was working, it was just a matter of time before I beat the odds and walked out of the hospital on my own two feet. "I knock, take your last draw." Kyle said as I was daydreaming. "What, that's not possible we just started." I replied as I picked my last card and discarded. "Let's see your hand." Kyle asked. He put his hand down and so did I, it turned out he did have thirty-one exactly and I had twenty-two. I wasn't even paying attention I was so excited about getting feeling back in my legs that I lost the game. "Want to play again or call it a night?" Kyle asked picking up the cards. Actually I wanted to continue to work on my therapy in private, I wanted to prove to Kyle that I wasn't going to give up and I could do it. "No, I think I'll turn in early. I'm tired from the work out session we had and I'd like to be ready for tomorrow." I replied to him. "Yeah, maybe we should call it a night we can play again another time. Besides I should be getting home myself. I'll be back in the morning and take you down stairs for the next session." He replied as he headed out the door.

I waited awhile to make sure Kyle was gone before I decided to make my move, I really wanted to see what I could do on my own. I couldn't get used to someone taking care of me for the rest of my life so I had to try to overcome being dependent on others. I was determined to succeed at everything I tried from here on in. I wasn't going to let anyone or anything stand in my way of success. I had to sneak past the nurses station and make my way downstairs to the therapy room without being seen, after all I couldn't explain how I managed to steal Kyle's key to the room without him realizing it. I slid myself into the chair and made my way past the nurse's station, luckily the nurse wasn't even near her post to notice anyone go by. This, I had never done before and it felt great to be sneaky for a change. On the other hand, If I get caught no telling what would happen after all I did steal the key from Kyle and that was theft but it was for a good cause. I knew they wouldn't see it that way because theft is theft no matter how you look at it. The risk was worth it to me I needed to do this and my time was running out, I wanted so bad to walk again I was willing to risk everything in order to make it happen. Once I made it to the room downstairs, I noticed no one was around except for the janitor, and he just said that he didn't see me and smiled. I guess I wasn't the only one who's tried something like this before.

I closed the door behind me and looked around, I wasn't sure where to start. Although I was sure the pool was out of the question for now. I decided to start on the leg lifts and made my way over to the incline board and slid out of the chair and lay down. I began slowly at first struggling to lift my legs with the pulley system that Kyle showed me earlier. The idea was to get my legs used to being forced to move, then release it and work it myself. I used the system for about twenty minutes before trying my luck. I strained myself hard and finally was able to lift my legs on my own I held them up for a time and then lowered them and continued to do it for as long as I could. The sweat was pouring off me and I knew it was all worth it, I knew it was working and I could feel my legs straining to work the way they once did normally. I worked for an hour before taking a rest and noticed a radio next to the table nearby. I needed some music right about now and wheeled myself over to turn it on when the janitor beat me to it. “How’s it going so far?” He said as he turned the radio on for me. “Great, I’m sorry for being here but I need to do this. Please don’t turn me in.” I answered. “I won’t. You’re not the first to try this and you won’t be the last, just stay away from the pool and be careful when no one else is in here with you.” He replied as he left. I thought he changed his mind and was going to turn me in, I guess some people realize that a person’s just got to take a chance sometime even if it’s wrong.

I was alone in the room once again and for a short time I just took a break and relaxed before getting started again. It was still early and I still had plenty of time to work out before the guard made his rounds. I knew the janitor wouldn’t turn me in, but if the guard caught me it would be all over for me. I listened to the radio and a song I knew well came on, I turned it up and felt the energy in the song flow threw me as though it was a part of me. Words couldn't fully describe the way the song motivated me to take on the world. I tried the uneven bars and tried to stand and see if I could force my muscles to walk. I held myself on my own two feet and moved one hand forward then the other trying to force my legs to do the same. At first it didn’t work but I kept trying hard. They wanted to move but my body wouldn’t listen to me. I sat back down and decided to work more on the leg lifts before I try again. For a time, all seemed hopeless but something inside me forced me to attempt to stand on my feet again. I forced myself to do it and finally was standing, I feared taking a step for I thought that I’d fall again. I finally got up the courage to try and move and succeeded, I took another step then another and it was like dragging lead weights but I was walking by myself very slowly so I wouldn’t fall. I tried hard to walk to the end of the room even though my legs felt weak, I pressed on determined more than ever not to quit until I was able to walk better.

I hadn’t noticed, but Kyle was watching me. Evidently I wasn’t as great a thief as I thought I was, I never did have any practice at it. I pressed on walking slowly up and down the room; I could feel my legs regaining the strength they once had before the accident. I couldn’t believe how great it felt to walk again. If only Kyle and Josh could see this I thought to myself as I continued my journey towards freedom. I couldn't wait to show Kyle that I did it, he believed in me when I almost gave up on myself. He too was a big part of my success of walking and I felt that I owed him. I never thought I'd find another friend that was willing to help me follow the right path in my life as Josh had done. I really wished that Josh were able to see me as I walked proudly as though it was the first time ever. My future began to have more meaning than ever before.

Before long the door opened and standing there was Kyle. My mouth dropped, I didn't know what to say or how to begin to explain. "I can explain all of this, I think." I said. "Don't worry about it, I noticed you taking my keys and figured you were up to something. How's it feel to be able to walk again?" Kyle replied. "It feels great. Except my legs still feel weak." I answered. I leaned against the post as I talked to him trying hard not to lose my balance. I wanted to stand as long as I possibly could; I realized then how much I had missed walking. "I knew you could do it. But you had to do it on your own. I could only be there to support you." Kyle said as he sat down. "I guess you were right. Do you think you could take me to Josh's grave tomorrow, I need to finally say good bye to my friend?" I asked. "Yeah, I don't for see any problem with that. I want you to use a cane for awhile for support, just to help you so you won't fall. You've come this far I'd hate to see you get injured further again." Kyle said to me. "Agreed, Besides I think I could use the extra support to walk while my legs get stronger." I said. I figured I was pretty lucky so at this point I wasn't about to go against his ideas.

Kyle and I headed back to my room, I held on to the hand railing as we walked real slowly to the elevator. That walk did tire me out; I could use the rest before I went to see Josh's gravesite. Josh and I had always been there for each other; it was that particular night that changed everything. I should've paid more attention to what Josh was saying but I didn't think he was serious enough to commit suicide. I still couldn't believe he was gone, we had so many plans I never thought they could all be taken away in the blink of an eye. Somehow, having Kyle around these last few days was like having a part of Josh still with me. Kyle encouraged me to try even though I still hurt inside, he said that life must still go on even though we miss the one's we care about. As the doors to the elevator opened, I thought about that night more and more. I missed him very much. "I know what you're thinking, It will hurt for some time I told you that before. This time you will not be going through it alone." Kyle said putting his hand on my shoulder leading me into the elevator. The doors closed like the lid on a coffin being shut forever, a thought I could only imagine was the last sight Josh's family saw of their son. I wanted to do the right thing but I couldn't deal with all the guilt that over came me that day, I blamed myself for his death and to this day I still feel partly to blame.

We made our way back to my room and Kyle suggested that we play cards again for a short time. "I was wondering are you planning on being around now that I'm on my feet again, or is this the end of it all?" I asked dealing the deck. I didn't want to lose another friend, especially one that reminded me of the one friend I hope I'd never forget. "That depends on whether or not you want to remain friends, hell I could use another good friend like anyone else." Kyle said as he discarded. "Then it's settled, friends?" I said reaching out my hand. Kyle shook my hand and that night we made a pact anytime we need each other, we're there for each other no matter where in the world we are. The game and conversation went on for more than three hours, it was like we were meant to be friends, and maybe this was the way things were always supposed to be. Josh once told me that things have a way of working out in the end, even if it's not the way we expect it to be it's usually for the best. "By the way, I finished it." I said as I handed him the finished copy of my book. "I knew you could do it. So what's the next step." Kyle asked leafing through the script. "The next step is to get it published, if it's good enough." I replied. I felt uneasy about the success of being able to become an author at such a young age. "It's good enough trust yourself and send it out. You've got nothing to lose." Kyle answered. "I hope you're right, I've worked hard on this and it would be great to get it published and become an author. It's been a dream of mine for some time." I said. "Dreams do come true if you want them bad enough." Kyle replied to me. With that we finished our game and said our good byes, but he decided to sleep in the next bed. He was too tired for the long drive home and felt it better just to stay seeing as how he'd be headed back here in about five hours. Anyway.

I slept through the night reflecting on how much I had achieved as well as how nervous I was at going to the gravesite. I felt as though Josh might hold me responsible somehow for not being the friend I should've been to him. I wasn't sure how to face up to the facts of what happened to him. It's true that Josh changed my life, I wouldn't be the person I was today if it weren't for him. I guess Kyle and I would have new path's to take.

I awoke late the next morning to find Kyle sitting in the chair wide-awake waiting for me to wake up. "Morning, its time to face your next fear today are you ready for it or what?" He asked me. I stretched out before answering him; my back was stiff maybe from pushing myself so much the night before. I sat up and just sat there for a time looking outside at the sun shining brightly. "I have to do it. I've waited too long as it is." I said to him. "It's never too late to face your demons, this is your chance to put it all behind you and start fresh it doesn't mean you have to forget all that the two of you did together. It just means that you have to go on with your life too." Kyle replied. Kyle was dressed and ready to go whenever I was; he was more than willing to help me through this, as a good friend would be. I put my feet on the cold floor and it felt great to feel the chill where I had no feeling before. I'll just get dressed and be right with you. I picked up my clean clothes and went to change.

A short time later I came out ready to go, Kyle held my cane in his hand waiting for me to take it. "It's only a crutch, something to lean on so you don't weaken to fast. Remember, It's been some time since you've walked so take it slow." Kyle said sternly. "You sound like my mother, don't worry the last thing I want is to go back to the chair again. It's time to be me for a change and make things happen for the right reasons." I answered him. I needed to continue the path that both Josh and I started together, it was the only way I could ever gain his forgiveness for the mistake I made of not being there for him when he needed me the most. A rush of memories flooded through my mind, it was as though I was able to relive all that we shared and a chance to see the difference we both made in each other's lives. I was forgiven.

We left the hospital; at around ten in the morning, along the way I just stared out the window looking at the world as though it was transparent. I felt like I was on the outside looking in at a world that was only a dream. I kept thinking I'd wake up and everything would be fine. The necklace that Josh had left me I wore proudly around my neck for the first time since the night of the funeral. I still remember the night I surprised him by buying it for him; he had always liked the way a bird flew so free through the air without knowing what was ahead of it. It was free the way Josh wanted to be himself. He got his wish the only way he knew how to and he did hurt those around him but not intentionally. "You're kind of quiet over there are you all right?" Kyle asked. "Yeah, I'm fine. I was just thinking about Josh. I wished I had more time to spend with him than I did." I answered. "You had what some would call a life time. Others aren't so lucky. Friends come and go and sometimes you just have to deal with the situation as it comes your way." Kyle replied. "How am I supposed to go on with out my friend, everytime I meet another friend I'll feel as though I betray a friendship that was to last a life time." I asked confused. "That's life. It just isn't fair. Maybe things do happen for a reason, I'm sure Josh would understand. No one can replace a friend that was lost. I'm not trying to replace Josh either." Kyle stated. The long drive came to an end as we pulled into the cemetery and parked the car as close to his grave as we could. "I guess this is it. I need to do this alone okay?" I asked him getting out of the car.

I made my way to the grave slowly using the cane that Kyle gave me as support. I noticed that the graveyard was well kept which showed that he was in a good place. I sat down beside his grave and sat in silence for a short time not knowing what to say, or where to begin. "I'm sorry it's taken me so long to get here. I miss you a lot Josh. I'm sorry I wasn't there when you really needed me, but I couldn't handle you leaving me the way you did. I was in an accident and nearly gave up on myself; I really needed you Josh. I did meet a great new friend that helped guide me back on the right path. If it weren't for him I wouldn't be here with you. He's a lot like you just as thick headed and stubborn. Even persistent when it comes to finishing something. We had so many plans Josh and I want to still go through with them, with Kyle that is." I said as I sat there as if he was sitting across from me. It did feel as though he was there listening to everything I was saying. "I don't want to be alone anymore Josh, I really need friends to be around and I need to get on with my life. I guess what I'm trying to say is that I'll always remember you and wish you were here with me. Please forgive me for that night. I still got the chain you left me and I'll never take it off, it's all I got left of you." I said as Kyle walked up behind me. I stood up and joined him as a tear rolled down my cheek. "You okay?" Kyle asked me. "Yeah, I think I'll be fine." I answered. As we started walking back to the car,

I felt as though I was no longer alone. I turned around just in time to see Josh himself standing near the stone smiling, I knew then that all was forgiven and I still had him as my best friend. I smiled back at him and he faded away as quickly as he appeared. I finally said good bye my friend.

Until this day I told no one of that incident, but it was true. Over time I managed to become the writer Josh always said I could be. My first book was published and I was very young at the time. Josh managed to change me even in death; I still use his spirit as a guide in all I do in life. Currently, I'm working on finishing my third book and hope it too will be as successful as the others. Kyle and I, well were still friends we even see each other often. I learned a lot about others and myself that summer. I realized that life is short and we have only one chance to make it in this world even though there will always be two paths in life to walk. The one we chose makes us who we really are in life. I have to be me. I knew for a fact that things were going to be okay.

ABOUT THE AUTHOR

James L. Edwards was born in 1970 and has lived all his life in Rhode Island. He has always believed that everyone has a destiny in life. This path in life has two directions; we must choose the right road to reach our goals even though both will always have many difficulties along the way.

Choose wisely, but remember no one is ever alone!

www.ingramcontent.com/pod-product-compliance
Ingram Content Group UK Ltd.
Pitfield, Milton Keynes, MK11 3LW, UK
UKHW041933190726
13854UKWH00004B/1558

9 780759 698406